KEEPING BAILEY

A FOREVER HOME NOVEL - BOOK 4

BY DAN WALSH

BAINBRIDGE PRESS

Keeping Bailey

Forever Home Series - Book 4

ISBN: 978-1-7341417-5-7

Published by Bainbridge Press

Cover design by Bainbridge Press

Cover photo: by Isaac Walsh (used with permission)

�֍ Created with Vellum

AUTHOR'S NOTE

I don't often write a note at the beginning of my novels but felt the need to do it with *Keeping Bailey*. It will be brief. I almost felt the need to include a hashtag on the book's cover (my wife talked me out of it). If I had, the hashtag would have said: *#TheDogLives.*

Like so many dog lovers, I don't really enjoy reading touching, even well-written dog stories where the dog featured in the story dies in the end. I know dogs do die. I've lived through it several times. It's always heartbreaking.

Here's some good news...*Keeping Bailey* is **not** about an old dog dying. Instead, the story addresses the need to stay true to our faithful friends as they age. So, rest assured... while there will be some suspenseful scenes (as there are in all my novels), Bailey will continue to be alive and well at the end of the book.

—Dan Walsh

1

Sandy Creek Area
Summerville, Florida

SOMETHING WAS DEFINITELY GOING ON. JUST WHAT, BAILEY couldn't quite figure out yet.

But she hadn't seen Harold this upset in a very long time. Not since Alice had left. She was the nice woman Harold had lived with ever since Bailey had been a pup. For most of Bailey's life—as long as she could remember—she had always been loved by both Harold and Alice together. When he didn't call her Alice, Harold called her *Sweetheart*. But he also called Alice "The Mother" sometimes, but only when she was doing something for Bailey, like feeding her or taking her for a walk.

"You wanna eat, Bailey?" he'd say. "The Mother's gettin' it. She's fixing it now."

Alice, The Mother, had always taken good care of Bailey.

Besides the food and walks, she'd kept her water bowl filled, brushed her, gave her baths sometimes, and lots of treats. Harold mostly loved on Bailey letting The Mother do everything else.

That is, until the day The Mother was gone. After that, Harold did all the things she used to do.

Whatever had happened that day, it must have been something awful. Harold cried and cried. Nothing Bailey did made it any better. The younger man who was here now had come over that day, too. Right after some people had taken The Mother away.

A few days later, the house filled up with scary strangers all dressed in dark clothes. All of them as sad as Harold. Even the young man who was here now. He wore dark clothes then, too.

Whoever he was, he and Harold were close. They hugged each other quite often. When he'd visit, Harold either called him "Son" or "Bill." On that day, Son was crying like Harold, right after they hugged. A short while later, Harold had shut Bailey up in his bedroom; the same room she'd slept in every night at the foot of their bed. She'd stayed there until everyone left.

That had suited Bailey just fine.

But today, Son wasn't wearing dark clothes, and he wasn't crying. But he did seem sad, though not as sad as Harold. They were sitting at the table talking, the smaller table closer to the kitchen. Bailey walked over and checked her water bowl. Mainly, she wanted to see if she could figure out more of what they were saying. See if they used any words she understood.

. . .

"Son, did you get anywhere calling your friends? Find anyone who can take Bailey?"

Bill sighed. He looked up at his father. Harold knew the answer before he spoke.

"I'm really sorry, Dad. I tried everyone I knew. Nobody can take her. Half of them live in places that don't allow dogs. The other half already own a dog, some more than one. But they all said they couldn't add another."

"Was it because of her age?" Harold said. "She's still really healthy. And smaller dogs like her can often live fifteen or sixteen years."

Bill shook his head. "I didn't even get that far. They all said no before her age ever came up. You know how it is with dogs...it's a big commitment. People aren't gonna say yes to something like that just to do a friend a favor."

Harold knew he was right. If circumstances were different, and one of his friends had asked him to take in one of their dogs, he'd have to turn them down, too. That had actually happened the year before Alice died. He and Alice both loved dogs. Problem was, Bailey didn't. She liked people. Most of them anyway. But she'd never warmed up to other dogs, no matter what their size, gender, or type.

"I'm really sorry," Bill said.

"I know. Appreciate how hard you tried." He looked down at Bailey, sitting by her water bowl, staring up at him with those amazing eyes. So full of kindness and concern. She was the sweetest thing on earth. Alice used to always make fun of all the names he'd give Bailey, all the things he'd say to her. "You know she doesn't understand 99% of the things you say." He'd tell Alice, "Maybe not, but she likes the way I say 'em."

How could he part with her?

No, he couldn't let himself go down that path. The decision had already been made. If Bill couldn't find her a new home, then he'd have to—

"I could bring her to the shelter for you, Dad. There's no reason you have to go."

Harold couldn't help it. Tears welled up in his eyes. "No, I'm gonna do it. I've got to. I at least owe her that after all the years she —" He couldn't finish the words.

Bill handed him a napkin, and he dabbed his eyes. Bailey quickly came over and snuggled up next to his leg. He reached down and patted her gently on the head.

"We don't have to do it today," Bill said. "If you're not ready. I can come back another day."

"No, we need to do it today. There's not going to be a better day. You're here now. I can't drive anymore. The van from the home will be here to move me the day after tomorrow. So, it has to be before then. The way my brain is slipping, I'm afraid to leave her alone here with me, as it is."

"Why, it's not like you're going to hurt her?"

"No, but I keep forgetting things. Like whether I fed her or not. Last night, I went to bed and forgot all about taking her out to the bathroom. The poor thing waited as long as she could, then literally started barking at me in bed until I figured out why."

Bill laughed. He reached down and scratched behind her ears. "You're a sweet girl, Bailey." He looked up at his dad. "Wish like crazy there was some way we could tell her what's going on, so she wouldn't be so confused."

"I know," Harold said. "That's the hardest part of this thing. Her thinking I'm just abandoning her for no reason." He looked down at her again but had to look away. "I'm clinging to one small consolation right now. Really two."

"What's that?" Bill said.

"I anticipated you might not be successful, so I put a call into that shelter we're bringing her to. Talked to a nice lady down there. Tried to explain the situation as best I could. Even sent her a picture of Bailey from my phone, so she could see what a fine dog she is. She told me, even with her age, they almost always find good homes for small dogs, especially ones as nice looking as Bailey."

"Well, see?" Bill said. "She's going to be okay, Dad. You don't have to feel bad about doing this. People are gonna take one look at that sweet little face and snap her right up. You'll see. You said there were two consolations you're clinging to. What's the other one?"

He looked up to the ceiling for just a second. "That this brain tumor's my ticket home. Won't be long now before the Lord puts me back with your mother. I'll miss Bailey something awful, but I've been missing your mom even more." He stood up on unsteady legs.

"You okay?"

"I'll be fine. Happens whenever I stand up too fast anymore. Let me get Bailey's leash on, and we'll take her for a ride down to that shelter now. Before I lose my nerve and change my mind."

. . .

BAILEY'S EARS perked right up. She'd been trying her best to figure out what Harold and Bill were talking about. Heard her name mentioned several times, so at least some of it was about her. She didn't pick up too much else.

But something good was happening now. Harold had just stood up and lifted her leash off its hook. Bill was standing, too. And she was quite sure she'd heard Harold use another familiar word...*Ride.*

They were going for a ride somewhere in the car. Bailey loved car rides almost as much as treats.

Look, he's putting on his coat.

2

Summerville Humane Society
Summerville, FL

KIM HARPER SAT AT HER DESK, HANDS ON THE KEYBOARD, awaiting inspiration to come from somewhere to help her write this article about an upcoming fundraiser for the local newspaper. There were days when newspapers would send out reporters to interview people like her and then go back to their newspaper office and write the story themselves. These were *not* those days.

Now, if her shelter was willing to write the article themselves and email it to the correct editor, they might consider cleaning it up and running it in the local section, hopefully before the event occurred.

As the Animal Behavior Manager, Kim wouldn't typically be given this assignment. But last week Tom Andrews, their Public Communications Director, had moved on—as he put it—to bigger and better things. Kim's boss had apologized after explaining that she would have to absorb these kinds of tasks until Tom's replacement could be found. Although it wasn't said, both understood the salary for Tom's job — since this was a nonprofit affair — was well below what it should have been.

Kim might be doing things like this for quite a while.

She glanced at her phone, hoping it would ring and free her from this assignment, if only for a few moments. It could happen. Ned, her boyfriend, sometimes called about now if he got his afternoon break. Although being a police officer did not lend itself to a predictable routine. But hearing his wonderful voice might be just the thing she needed to help her write this piece. Ned always had such great ideas.

"I'm sorry."

Kim heard a familiar chair squeak and turned to face Amy, her friend and coworker. "For what?" Kim said.

"That they stuck you with Tom's work," Amy said. "They knew better than to ask me. I'm such a lousy writer."

Kim smiled. "You really are. But you're a wonderful person, and that's more important. And you've become a first-rate dog trainer. And that's what we need you for, not writing publicity articles for fundraisers."

As if sensing Amy's sympathy toward Kim, Finley got up from beside Amy's desk and came over. He rested his adorable face on her lap and gave her a look that said, "Everything will be all right." Kim patted his head and scratched behind his ears. "Thanks for the love, Finley. You're such a good boy." She looked at Amy. "I thought today was Chris's day to take Finley to work." Chris was Amy's husband, a groundskeeper at the local golf club.

"It was supposed to be his day," Amy said. "But they're trying something new. Ever since Chris started working there, the golf pro had been giving him free lessons. He's a vet like Chris, and he felt sure he could help Chris come up with a decent golf swing, even with his prosthesis. Turns out, he was right. Apparently, Chris is a natural. I watched him a couple weekends ago. He really creams that ball now. But Chris said even his short game is starting to come together. So, the pro asked Chris if he would consider teaching golf to a group of kids with physical challenges. The two of them are meeting with these kids this afternoon. The golf pro felt like, with Chris's leg situation and him being a vet, the kids would really respond well to him."

"That's wonderful, Amy. It's amazing how far Chris has come since he first came out here to work with Finley. So, is he going to do this from now on, instead of taking care of the grounds?"

"No," Amy said. "This class will be just once a week. But I could tell the way he talked about it at breakfast this morning, he's hoping it could turn into more."

"Well, tell him how happy I am for him." She looked down at Finley. "And you sir can go back and lay down. I'm really doing just fine."

Her telephone rang.

As soon as she saw it, she knew it couldn't be Ned. He always called on line three. Lines one and two were always in-house. "Hello, Kim Harper speaking."

"Hey Kim, this is Nancy over here at Intake. Sorry to do

this, but we have a situation here that could use your expertise."

Kim remembered, Nancy was new and still in training. "Can you speak freely?"

"Yeah," Nancy said, "the dog owners are in the interview room. They can't hear me."

"So, what's going on?"

"Basically, it's an old dog situation. I'm still terrible at handling these. As soon as I see the dog's face, I just lose it. They have no idea what's about to happen, and I get so upset at these dog owners. I'm afraid I'll say the wrong thing. I know you've tried to help me do better with these, but I...I'd really feel better if you were here. Maybe if I saw you handle it one more time, it would stick. Would you mind?"

Kim smiled. She probably disliked these old dog surrenders just as much as Nancy did. Oddly enough, though, Nancy's request was still preferable to writing this fundraising article. "I'll be right down."

3

KIM DID HER BEST TO AVOID TOO MANY ENTANGLEMENTS AS she made her way through the shelter to the Intake area. Part of her job was to answer questions from staff members, and she especially enjoyed taking time with the newer ones. She told a few of them she'd get back to them as soon as she handled this pressing situation for Nancy.

When she got there, Nancy met her by the front counter. "They're still in the interview room. I got the paperwork here if you decide you're okay with them surrendering their dog. But I'm really hoping you can work your magic in there."

Kim smiled. "I don't know about doing any magic. With some people, nothing works. So, bring those forms with you just in case." She walked toward the interview room then paused. "Any more details you want to tell me first?"

Nancy sighed. "Seems to me it's just a family wanting to trade in their old model for a new one. Kind of what my ex did with me. But that's another story. They're saying the dog doesn't have any health issues that they know of. When you hear their reasons for turning him in, try not to slap 'em. The urge was certainly there for me."

Kim smiled again. Nancy had quite a sense of humor, but Kim wondered if her social skills weren't up to the level needed to work the Intake area. Not her call to make, though. Kim opened the door. At the head of the table sat a woman in her late thirties, hair rolled up in a makeshift bun. No makeup, wearing a tan shirt with a flowery pattern. Beside her sat a dark-haired teenage boy in a T-shirt and jeans, staring at his phone. Lying beside him against the wall was a Lab-mix, male dog with short brown hair. He was looking at the boy but quickly turned to face Kim. His tail started thumping, and he gave her a good-old-boy smile. She could see the graying hair in his face, but he had the friendliest eyes.

Kim walked around the table to greet the dog first. "And who do we have here?" She bent down and began to pet him.

"That's Rex," the woman said. "Hate to do it, but feels like it's time. Been thinking about it for weeks."

"I'm Kim Harper, by the way. The Animal Behavior Manager here at the shelter."

"Can't the other gal take Rex without your say-so?"

"It's not quite like that, but they like to call me in sometimes to assess a situation. Surrendering a dog is a big step. Like you said, you've been thinking about it for weeks. Does Rex have any health issues? Like some major vet bills coming up? That have anything to do with your decision to bring him down here today?"

"Oh, no. Nothing like that. He's just old, is all. Doesn't hear as well as he used to."

"Is he starting to...go backwards on his housebreaking?" Kim said. "You know, having accidents in the house?"

"No, nothing like that, either. We gotta doggy door in the kitchen, let's out to a fenced-in backyard. He still knows his way in and out of there."

"Has he started to become aggressive? Like, with children? He seems perfectly fine with your son here." Kim took notice that the boy hadn't even lifted his eyes from his phone since she walked in.

"No," the woman said. "Rex don't have a mean bone in his body." Hearing his name, got his tail thumping again. He looked up at the woman with all kinds of love on his face. "But the kid situation was my main tipping point for bringing him down. We got him as a pup when Rodney here was little. He used to pay all kinds of attention to him. He and Rex would play out in the backyard, do all kinds of things together. But as you can see, Rodney's grown now, and between his friends, his PlayStation, and that stupid phone, he ain't got no time for Rex."

Rodney looked up from his phone just long enough to roll his eyes at his mom.

"I got remarried a few years back, took possession of my new husband's two kids. They're home with him at the moment. They never had a dog before, and me and my husband been talking about maybe it's time to get them a puppy of their own. Old Rex here, he's got no energy for little kids. They'll go out in the backyard when he goes out to do his business, and throw a ball for him. Rex just looks at it like, *What do you want me to do about it?* He's just too old to play. Not his fault. It's just life, I guess. But we don't think it's fair to these two younger ones to have to wait for old Rex to up and die before they get their chance to experience a puppy. You follow me? We figure Rex might be better off getting with some old retired folks, you know? People who may be living at the same energy level he is."

Kim looked over at Nancy, who gave her a mild shrug.

"Something wrong with my thinking?" the woman said. "Seems like it's the best solution for everyone, including Rex. He could be with someone that really wants him. You know, like a lonely widow, or something. Just looking for a little company."

What Kim was about to say wasn't easy for her. Before she'd understood these situations better, she might've thought this woman had a point. Almost any life might be better for Rex than being totally ignored in a home like this. But that's not how Rex would see it. And this woman's expectations needed some gentle adjustment.

Gentle, Kim reminded herself. *She thinks she's doing Rex a favor.*

"You asked a moment ago," Kim began, "whether something was wrong with your thinking. The honest answer is... yes. But I can see why you might think this is the right solution. The problem is, Rex won't interpret what you're planning the way you think he will. Right now, he seems supremely content, even though he's in a strange situation. You might be thinking, that's just how he is, and how he'll be once you get up and leave. But it's not."

"No?" the woman said.

Kim shook her head. "Not even close. He's content now — believe it or not — because you're here. And even because Rodney's here, even though Rodney hasn't paid him any attention." For the first time, Rodney looked up for more than a few seconds. "See, to Rex, you guys are his whole life. You're at the center of all his memories. When he sees Rodney, a part of him might wish Rodney would treat him the way he used to. But he's probably okay with how things have changed. He has great memories of all those times Rodney *used* to play with him. And seeing Rodney, just seeing him, makes Rex happy." Kim looked right into the woman's eyes. "Seeing *you* makes Rex happy. I'll bet you're the one who always feeds him and changes his water. The one who's probably taken him to the vets whenever he needed to go, helped calm him down whenever he was scared."

Tears welled up in the woman's eyes. Kim saw the boy swallow hard. He wasn't looking at his phone anymore.

"That's why Rex is so calm right now," Kim said. "Because the two people who matter most in his life are right here in this room. If you walk out that door and leave him here, everything he cares about, everything that matters to him goes with you. And all he'll be wondering for days, maybe weeks, when you're coming back to get him. He might not eat. He probably won't wag his tail when people check him out in his pen. He won't look anything like he does now. He'll just sit in the back of that pen as depressed as can be, unable to process why he's been left alone like this. A dog in that condition is pretty hard to adopt out to anyone. And you'd be surprised, how few retired people come in here looking for a dog Rex's age. And for those who might come, if he's too sad to even greet them..."

Tears rolled down the woman's cheeks. The boy's, too, but he quickly wiped them on his sleeve. Nancy got out of her chair, reached for a box of tissues on the windowsill. She used the first one to dab her own eyes.

"I don't want that," the woman said, reaching for the tissue box. "Not for Rex. He's been way too good a dog to let him end up that way. But what can we do? My husband's expecting us to get a puppy for his kids. And I don't think I got it in me to say everything to him, the way you just said it to us."

Rodney took out a tissue, too. "I don't want that for Rex, neither."

"Well," Kim said, "the good news is, you really don't have to choose one or the other. In general, how does Rex get along with other dogs?"

"He's good with other dogs," Rodney said. "Long as they're friendly."

"That's good," Kim said. "If you plan to get your puppy from here, I can help you make the situation work. We can follow some steps to make sure the puppy you pick will be a good fit for Rex. I can help you train him, or her. Even work with the children in the training. The main thing will be not to expect too much from Rex. He won't mind all the attention the new pup's getting from your kids. He'll be happy just to watch from afar. The main thing will be to keep the puppy from bothering Rex too much. But other than that, sounds like he'll do just fine."

The woman's whole expression changed. So did her son's. "I think we can manage that," she said. "What do you think, Rodney?"

"Definitely," he said. He reached down and acknowledged Rex for the first time directly. "Here that boy? You're not going anywhere. You're coming back home with us."

Rex stood up for that and leaned into Rodney's leg, his tail just wagging back and forth.

"I can't thank you enough, Miss..." The woman held out her hand.

"It's Kim." She shook her hand. "Happy to help. And seriously, you go make sure things are okay with your husband. If he has any questions, feel free to call. When you're ready, come on back and we'll set up a meet-and-greet with Rex and your new puppy."

"Thank you, Kim. Thank you so much."

Kim backed out of the interview room, followed by Nancy. The woman and her son went out into the hall and back outside toward the parking lot.

"C'mon, Rex," the boy said. "Wanna go for a ride?"

Nancy watched the scene unfold, turned to Kim and said, "See...it is magic. There's no way I could ever pull off something like that."

4

RHONDA HAWTHORNE WAS PRETTY EXCITED. LAST WEEK, SHE had finally made the decision to get off her duff and do something meaningful with her life. So, she'd responded to an invitation from Connie, her next door neighbor, to attend an orientation meeting at the Summerville Humane Society. They were looking for volunteers to come work at the shelter a few days a week. Connie had signed up several months ago and loved it, so she'd been bugging Rhonda to give it a try.

Rhonda and Connie lived side-by-side for the last seven years at Colony in the Wood, a 55-plus village of manufactured homes in Summerville. That's when Rhonda had moved in with her husband, Ted. She had just retired after being a public school teacher for thirty years. They didn't need the big house they'd raised their kids in anymore, so these cute little cottages at Colony fit the bill nicely. Connie had already moved in her place a few years before that.

Then suddenly, a year later and without any warning, Rhonda's husband Ted died from a massive heart attack. They didn't even know he had heart problems before that, hadn't been taking any heart medication, wasn't overweight. But there she was, only sixty-two, living life as a widow. Connie had been such a comfort to her then and ever since. She'd been a widow for over five years. Rhonda soon learned the park had its fair share of widows. And although there were plenty of social activities available to Rhonda, lots of ladies in similar circumstances, she never quite felt ready to jump in. "I'm just not a joiner," she'd tell Connie whenever she'd extend an invitation.

But then three months ago, Amos, Rhonda's beloved cockapoo died. He was a wonderful companion and did a great job keeping Rhonda from feeling too lonely after Ted died. Ted's the one who got him, had surprised Rhonda one day when he'd brought him home as a pup.

At first, Rhonda wasn't sure how she'd make it living by herself, but she was too heartbroken about Amos to even think about getting another dog. It took a while, but she'd finally adjusted to life on her own and decided maybe it was best just to keep things like that from now on. The problem was, she liked dogs. She and Ted had owned one for most of the years they'd been married. She was talking about this with Connie last week out on the porch. Connie suggested she try volunteering at the shelter.

"They really need the help down there," Connie had said. "And you get to be around dogs the whole time, but you don't have to make any commitment. You pick your hours, what days you want to come in. The dogs love getting the attention, and it helps them get adopted quicker because they're staying connected to people, so they respond better when people come in to pick out a dog."

So, Rhonda said yes. And today was the day. She picked up her purse and her sweater, locked the front door, and headed next door to meet Connie, who was already standing in her driveway by her car.

"You ready?" Connie said.

"Ready as I'll ever be, I guess."

"You're gonna love it. I just know it."

"I am pretty excited," Rhonda said. "Feels good to be doing something useful."

"It's definitely that," Connie said. "But it's also a lot of fun."

THEY PULLED into the parking lot at the shelter, closest to the door where the orientation class was being held. Connie knew her way around the facility very well. On the drive over, she'd told Rhonda that after dropping her off at the multi-purpose room, she wouldn't be staying for the class but doing her regular volunteer work. However, Rhonda shouldn't be surprised to see Connie make an appearance at some point. She'd already been asked to come in by Kim Harper, the Animal Behavior Manager, to help with a demonstration.

Rhonda came into the spacious room to find about a dozen other would-be volunteers spread out among three rows of folding chairs. At the front, there was a metal podium and a desk to the right. Behind them, a white screen. Rhonda took her seat and noticed that all but two of the volunteers were women, and all looked to be of retirement age.

A red-haired woman dressed smartly in business attire came in, stood behind the podium, and opened up a file folder. As if flipping a switch, she looked out over the attendees and flashed a big smile. "Good afternoon, ladies...and you two brave gentlemen. We're always grateful to have men become a part of our volunteer crew. My name is Alyssa Matthews, and I'm the Volunteer Coordinator here at the shelter. So, if you do decide to sign up — which you can do at the end of today's session — we'll be spending a lot more time together in the days ahead."

Alyssa went on to share some other opening remarks, gave a brief history of the Summerville shelter, highlighted some of the various ways volunteers could serve, then shared a slide showing the various members of the management and staff they might be interacting with. Rhonda noticed on the second row a picture of Kim Harper, the woman Connie had talked about in the car. No sooner had she done this, when Alyssa singled Kim out in her remarks.

"Pay particular attention to that young lady on the second row, Kim Harper. Next to me, she'll probably be the management person you'll spend the most time with. In fact, she'll be coming in here in just a minute to share some important information with you all."

After a few more remarks, a side door opened and in walked Kim Harper. Alyssa turned to face her and said, "And here she is, our Animal Behavior Manager, Kim Harper." She stepped aside to allow Kim to take the podium.

Rhonda thought she was much more attractive than the photo gave her credit for. Younger looking, too. Rhonda guessed she could easily be the same age as her daughter, Anna. Kim also smiled as she greeted everyone, but her smile didn't seem forced or manufactured. Within the first few moments, you could tell this young lady knew her stuff and felt totally at ease speaking in public.

"As Alyssa mentioned, I get to work with our volunteers quite a bit. My job — I guess you could say — is something of a specialization. My area of expertise is understanding how animals think, especially dogs. Cats think also, as anyone can plainly see, by the interesting expressions on their faces." Everyone laughed. "But cats as a rule are more guarded with their secrets."

"They think they're better than us," one of the men said. "Like we're here to do their bidding."

"An obvious dog lover," Kim said. Everyone laughed again. "Although what you said could possibly be true. Some of their behavior does seem to suggest at least some cats do hold this view. The jury is still out on that. But dogs are much more transparent in the way they attempt to communicate with us, and with each other. We've been able to study their behavior for years now and have learned so much about how to read what a dog is thinking, feeling, and trying to communicate. It involves way more than barking and tail-wagging. I don't have time to get into all of this now, but it is why I am often brought into situations here at the shelter. For example, I'm responsible to pick out the dogs we might bring to one of our fundraising events. At all of these events we need many volunteers to help us with the dogs, before, during, and after."

"That's actually one of the things I'm wanting to sign up for," the lady beside Rhonda said. "Special events, like that Summerville Family Days event at the city center last month."

"Glad to hear it," Kim said. "Hope quite a few of you will sign up for that. Of course, as volunteers, it's totally up to you. That can be the only way you help us out. Or, we hope many more of you might also sign up for our most-needed task, which is dog walking."

"That's why I'm here," another woman said.

"Good," said Kim."

Rhonda wanted to say *me, too*, but held her peace.

"It is so essential," Kim continued, "for the dogs already approved for adoption to interact with people, as often as possible. Believe it or not, whatever happened in these dogs' lives that brought them here, they are very traumatized by it. Not that they are ever treated badly once they get here. Just the opposite. We do everything we can to help them. But nothing can replace the time and attention they get when our volunteers come and take them out for a walk, or maybe play with them in the fenced-in areas. It helps them to want to connect with people again, which is so important when people come looking for a dog to adopt. They want to see dogs looking happy and eager to be petted, not hiding in the back of their pens all depressed and sad."

The side door opened again and in walked Rhonda's friend, Connie, holding the leash of a big black dog. Connie scanned the crowd for Rhonda, smiled and waved, as she walked toward Kim.

"Here's one of our most devoted dog-walking volunteers now. Folks, this is Connie. And who do we have here with you, Connie?"

"This is Mack," Connie said. "He's been here at the shelter for a few weeks now. The first time I saw him, he was nothing like this. He was sitting in the back of his pen, sad as can be. As you can see, Mack is totally different now. He loves to interact with people."

Just then, the side door opened again. A woman dressed like a staff worker poked her head in halfway and motioned to Kim, as if she had an urgent message. Kim nodded to her then looked back at the class.

"Okay folks, I've asked Connie if she wouldn't mind demonstrating our dog walking protocols, with Mack's help of course. For those who are only interested in working with cats and other smaller animals, you can follow Alyssa out the main door. She'll take you to a nearby room and explain the kinds of ways you can help us there." She looked at the woman still standing in the side doorway. "Let me just connect with Nancy here for a minute, and I'll be right back."

As she heard Connie take over the meeting, Kim headed toward Nancy and could instantly tell from her eyes something was wrong. It even looked like she might have been crying. She stepped into the hallway and closed the door.

"What's wrong, Nancy?"

"I'm SO sorry to do this, but I didn't know what else to do. We've got another situation in Intake—another old dog surrender—but this one's nothing like the one you took care of a little while ago. After hearing the backstory, I almost completely lost it. It's just way over my head. Would you mind coming by to see what you think?"

Kim looked at her watch. "My part of the orientation class is almost over. Can you stall them for five minutes?"

"Yeah," Nancy said. "I'm sure that'll be fine. Thanks." She turned and headed back toward the Intake area.

5

KIM MADE HER WAY OVER TO THE INTAKE AREA IN FAIRLY GOOD spirits. Every single one of the people who'd taken the orientation class had signed up to become a volunteer. Always great to have fresh help joining the team. But now, she found herself tensing up as she rounded the corner and saw Nancy up ahead. Not just because of what Nancy had said, but her demeanor. With the last situation, she had wanted to slap the folks who wanted to turn in their old dog. Whatever this was, she'd said she had almost lost it when she realized what was going on.

"Okay, Nancy. I'm here. What are we looking at?"

Nancy looked up, released a deep sigh. "It's just awful, Kim. Pretty much the opposite situation you helped me with a little while ago. I don't see any way out of this one."

"Okay...tell me about it."

"It's an elderly father and his son. The father's not actually in here, but I saw him out by the car when he handed off the dog to his son. He's the one who brought her inside. Kim, it was just so sad. The dad was just sobbing. And as he walked away, back to his car, the little dog was pulling at the leash trying to get back to him. But he kept walking and didn't look back. I opened the door to see if everything was all right just in time to hear the dad yell over his shoulder to his son, that he couldn't do it. He couldn't face it and would his son please take her inside for him. He barely got the words out through his tears. The son turns to face me with a dog on the leash, and his eyes are full of tears. I haven't even heard the whole story yet, and I'm getting choked up."

"Is the dad still out there now?" Kim said.

"Yeah, but I haven't talked with him. The son came in and told me what was going on, but he was so upset. Said he'd never seen his dad cry like that except when his mother died. He had to carry the dog inside. She wouldn't come in on the leash."

"What kind of dog is it?"

"It's really nice looking. He said it was a mini-Aussie. Her name's Bailey. She's eleven and in pretty good health. On heartworm prevention meds, had all her shots. No fleas or skin issues."

"Wow, eleven," Kim said.

"You can see the age on her face a little, but she was so distressed, seeing the old man so upset. And the son, too, although he said he's not very close to the dog. He's mostly doing this as a favor to his dad."

"And why is the dad surrendering the dog?"

"Doesn't have a choice," the son said. "He's had Bailey since she was a pup. He and his wife, but then she died last year. And now he's got an inoperable brain tumor, so they're having to move him into a home in a couple of days that doesn't take dogs. The son said he can't have dogs where he lives, he's tried all his father's friends. He only brought her here as a last resort."

"Are they in the interview room?"

Nancy nodded. "I left the paperwork there with the son, so he could start filling it out. Hope that's okay, but I didn't know what else to do."

"That's fine. Doesn't sound like we have many options here."

"Do you mind if I let you handle this one without me?" Nancy said, "I don't think I could sit through another round of him replaying all the details."

"Don't worry," Kim said, "I'll handle it. But I'm going to do my best to keep the son from having to go through everything all over again with me."

Kim walked down the hall, paused before opening the door, and said a little prayer.

She walked in to find a visibly distressed man in his mid-fifties comforting a small dog with a thick black coat lying on the table. She was huddled up near his chest, and she was panting. Judging by some other factors Kim knew she was probably more distressed than the son.

"I hope this is okay having her up here," he said. "But she was just too upset on the floor, constantly begging to be picked up."

"That's totally fine, sir. My name is Kim Harper. I'm the Animal Behavior Manager here at the shelter. Obviously, this is a difficult time."

"I'll say. Way more than I was expecting. My name's Bill. I filled out these forms and signed them. I'm hoping we can speed this along. I really don't like leaving my father out there in the car alone, considering his condition."

"I understand. This should only take a few more minutes. You don't need to go over all the details. My associate filled me in pretty well. But just a couple of things to make sure I don't miss anything important. As far as you know, Bailey has no health issues?"

"No. My dad said, other than being a little hard of hearing, she's in good shape for an old dog."

"Do you know how she is with children, or with other dogs?"

"Not great on either score, I'm afraid. Dad says she's always been afraid of other dogs. She used to be good with kids, back when our kids were small, and we got over there more often. But now kids make her almost as nervous as other dogs do."

"Is she on any special diet?"

"I don't know if you'd call it special, but my dad wrote out a page of the food she's been eating, how often, and some of her other...peculiarities. I put it under the forms there and even left a partially-opened bag of dog food out there at the desk. See, this is really tearing him up. He wouldn't have done this, bring her here I mean, if there was any way he could keep her. But the doctors are saying he's going to start going downhill pretty fast, and he didn't want Bailey here to pay the price. You know, he's forgetting things. Losing his balance more and more. He was afraid, what if he suddenly died with just him and Bailey in the house? He wanted to make sure she'd be looked after once he was gone. What do you think the chances are for her? Finding a new home, I mean?"

Kim didn't want to overstate things, so she said, "We will do the very best we can. She's eleven, but dogs her size can often live to be fifteen or sixteen. And she's a nice looking dog, so that will help. And even though she's upset, I can tell she has a sweet face."

"She really is sweet," Bill said. "My dad always says she's the sweetest thing on earth."

"Will she let me pet her?" Kim said. "Maybe get a little closer?"

"Oh sure. She might not like kids that much, but she loves people. Especially nice ones."

Kim moved to the chair next to Bill and began to pet her and talk to her gently. She could feel Bailey shaking, but she responded well to the attention. "What a nice girl you are, Bailey. And such a pretty face."

Her little nub of a tail began to wag. Kim continued to comfort her and pet her. As she did, Bill began to back away, then stood up slowly. Kim, realizing what he was attempting, moved over to his chair and continued to pet and talk to Bailey calmly.

"If you're okay with this," Bill said, "I'm just going to slip out of here and close the door behind me."

"That'll be fine, Bill. I'll just stay with her here a few more minutes. She really is so sweet."

He made his way to the door, opened it quietly, and looked back. His eyes were full of tears, and he mouthed the words, "Thank you."

"Bailey and I will be just fine. Won't we girl?"

BAILEY WAS SO TIRED. She didn't understand anything that was happening. Harold was so upset, and she didn't know why. He went back to the car, but Bill wouldn't let her help him. He needed her, she could tell, but instead, Bill picked her up and brought her into this room. She could tell he was upset, too. That and being in such a strange place made her so nervous, she couldn't stop shaking. Now Bill had left, and this nice woman was here. Bailey was sure she had never seen this woman before. But there was something about her that she liked. Something soothing about the way she talked, and her hands were so gentle.

Bailey was actually starting to feel sleepy.

Maybe if she slept a little while, when she woke up, Harold would be here to take her back home.

6

THREE DAYS LATER

KIM STEPPED into her office to find Amy banging away at the keyboard. She looked but didn't see Finley anywhere. "Finley with Chris today at the golf course?"

"He is," Amy said. "I don't know what Chris does with him all day, but whatever it is, Finley really likes it. He gets way more excited on mornings when he gets to go with him to work."

"I feel bad about Parker sometimes," Kim said. "Obviously, he's way too small to be a K-9 police dog, so there's no chance Ned could ever take him with him to work. If we were married and lived in the same place, I could bring him here with me most days." She sat at her desk. "As it is, he's got the same kind of life as most dogs whose owners work. Home by themselves most of the day."

"Doesn't that little boy, Russell, who lives next door to Ned, come stay with Parker after school?"

"He does, at least three days a week. So, he gets a little break then. But he'd be a great little dog to have here in the office. He's almost as well-trained as Finley. I've been working with him ever since Ned and I started dating."

Amy stopped typing and turned to look at Kim. "You two been dating a while now. I know a girl doesn't say things like, *if we were married,* unless they've been thinking about getting married. Are you pretty settled that Ned's the one?"

Kim smiled. "I've been settled on that for several months now. I'm just waiting for him to pop the question. Every now and then, he says things that make me think it's going to happen soon, but...still waiting."

"So, you no longer have any misgivings?" Amy said, "about Ned's line of work? I know when you two first got together, you were struggling with that."

"You mean when he almost got killed stopping that robbery? Yeah, that did give me some pause. But after some prayer and getting some good advice, I was able to get to a better place. It helps that we live in such a small town. There hasn't been anything even remotely as dangerous as that incident since then. Some of Ned's police friends who've been at it way more years than him, told me they've never been shot at before and think it's highly unlikely he'll get into such a sticky situation like that anytime soon."

"I think we're also fortunate," Amy said, "that none of that anti-police drama you see on the news sometimes has ever surfaced here."

Kim was glad about that, too. Although when it did

make the news, she knew it really bothered Ned. Once he'd explained to her all the proactive reforms they'd put in place in Summerville and how well they had worked as a result. He wished the same kinds of things could be implemented in many of these big cities.

"So, I've got just one more question," Amy said. "Since you're so ready to say yes if Ned pops the question, and you think he's been close several times, why don't you do it?"

"Ask Ned to marry me? Or ask him to ask me?"

"Either one."

"I'm way too old-fashioned for that."

"That's what I figured," said Amy. "I probably am, too, though Chris asked way before we got that far." Amy made a face, like she got a bright idea. "Why don't you try this? Bring up the fact how Chris and I take turns bringing Finley to work with us, and that you know he can't do something like that with Parker. But you could...but only *if* you were both living at the same place. That may give him the idea to finally —"

"I can't do that, Amy. But thanks for trying. I'm just gonna wait until Ned is ready."

"But what if he's one of these guys that doesn't mind dating for fifteen years?"

Kim laughed. "Then that would be terrible. But he's not like that. I'm sure he's not. For one thing, this isn't one of those *Friends With Benefits* deals. We're both Christians, and we've already had that conversation. We're waiting till we get married, like the Bible says. See, even that. We had that conversation, and we even used the M-word."

"Did you use it, or did Ned use it?" Amy said.

Kim thought about it. "No, Ned used it. It was on one of our first dates when he dropped me off at my apartment. He knew I was a Christian already, and I knew he was. So, he thought we should clear the air. He really wanted to kiss me good night but thought I shouldn't ever ask him to come inside, not after a date anyway. And I told him I thought that was a good idea. One thing could lead to another, then another. And he said, he wanted to wait for that part of our relationship until we were married."

"He said that?" Amy asked, all excited.

"Yes, that's what he said."

"You mean, just like that. *I want to wait for that part of our relationship until we are married.*"

"Yes," Kim said. "Why are you getting so excited? You told me you and Chris waited till your wedding night, too."

"I know," Amy said. "But if Ned said it *that* way, he all but asked you to marry him. That night. You should have jumped on that and asked, *And when might that be Ned?*"

Kim looked at Amy. "Amy, can you see me doing something like that? Does that even sound like something I would ever do?"

"Guess not. Maybe if this turned into something like fifteen years."

"It's not. Let's just drop the subject. One of these days — and I don't think years from now — I'll come into this office like I did this morning, my face beaming like the sun, holding out my hand with a ring on it. Until that day, there will be no scheming, or nagging, or coercion. Just old-fashioned stuff. Me being patient, focusing on my job. Like we both need to be doing now."

"Okay, boss," Amy said. "Speaking of our jobs. How's that little dog doing that got dropped off a few days ago? You know, the older one. The one that got you so upset."

Kim sighed. "You mean, Bailey?"

"That's the one."

"I was just checking on her before I came in here. She's not doing well at all. Still just curled up in the back of her pen, as depressed as can be. She's barely eaten a thing since she came. She looks up at me when I call her, but only for a second then looks away."

Kim knew there was only one face Bailey wanted to see on the other side of that gate. Sadly, she would probably never see that face again. And there was no way to help her understand why.

7

RHONDA WAS PRETTY UPBEAT AS SHE CAME OUT HER FRONT door, turned and locked it. She glanced over at Connie's, didn't see her yet. Today was Rhonda's first day volunteering at the shelter. Connie was going over, too, so they decided to drive together in Connie's car. She walked across the lawn between their two places, waved at Margaret Simpson as she rode by on her tricycle. It was a beautiful Florida morning, nice and sunny, uncommonly low humidity. Good day to be outside, where she planned to be shortly, walking dogs at the shelter.

She stood by the car for a few minutes but didn't see any signs of Connie moving about through the living room windows. She walked in through Connie's screen room, then up the couple of steps through her side door into the kitchen. That's the kind of relationship they had. "Connie, you coming?"

"I'm in here, Rhonda. Back in the bedroom. Sent you a text, but I guess you didn't see it."

Rhonda walked down the hallway and stood in the open doorway of the master bedroom. There was Connie, sitting up in bed leaning against some pillows. Her TV was on in the corner.

"Coming down with something," she said. "Might just be my allergies acting up, but I'm all congested and got a runny nose."

Rhonda wasn't too worried it was something serious like COVID, since they'd both gotten the vaccine. "Sorry to hear that. I didn't even look at my phone."

"But you don't need me, right?" Connie said. "They showed you what to do at the end of the orientation meeting. You know, signing in at the desk and what-not."

"They did. But I was still hoping we'd go in there together. Kind of counting on you to show me the ropes. You know, like knowing which dog to pick for the walk."

"Well, they all need walking. There's a chance some volunteers got there as soon as the place opened up, already took some of the dogs out and back again. But the gal who works on staff in that area can show you which dogs haven't had a turn yet."

"Okay," Rhonda said, "what about the size issue? Remember my hip? I can't walk big dogs unless they're well-trained and don't pull."

"That shouldn't be a problem," Connie said. "Mainly because they separate the dogs by size. Just tell the girl you can only walk smaller dogs, and she'll bring you to that part of the kennel where the small dogs are. Most of the dogs haven't been trained yet. Not by Kim anyway. She'll usually get involved training the dogs once they've been adopted. With small dogs, it won't really matter. Even if they pull, they don't weigh enough to do any damage. But eventually, you can ask Kim if she'll give you some tips on how to train a dog to walk right. She's got a technique that works very well, even on big dogs."

"All right, I might just do that...eventually. For now, I'll just stick with the small dogs. Is there anything I can get you at the store while I'm out?"

"Nope, I'm all set. Got my water bottle here, and my remote. You go on and have fun. The folks there are so nice. They'll make you feel right at home."

"Okay then, hope you feel better."

RHONDA PULLED into the shelter parking lot, had no problem finding an open space. Off to the left, she saw the big fenced-in area where volunteers were supposed to walk the dogs, always on a leash of course. Since she wasn't there by appointment, she decided to head over to the fence and see if anyone was already doing it. Sure enough, she saw two men and a lady walking dogs on the far side around the perimeter, separated by half a football field. That's the language they had used in the class to provide enough separation so that the dogs would not be totally focused on other dogs in the area. With some dogs, they'd said, you might need even more distance than that.

But the dogs she watched seemed to be doing just fine. Two big ones and a smaller one. The dogs weren't walking

perfectly beside the volunteer, but nobody's shoulder
seemed to be getting yanked out of joint. On either end,
within the huge area, were two smaller fenced-in zones
about the size of an average backyard. She remembered
these were mostly used for people considering a dog adoption, to give them a nice place to spend some time getting to
know the dog they were considering.

A young couple was sitting on a bench in the area on
her right, petting a mid-sized brownish dog. The young
man threw a ball toward the far end of the fence. Rhonda
had to laugh. The dog watched the ball roll to a stop in the
grass but didn't move an inch. "Hope fetching isn't a dealbreaker for them," she said to no one.

She walked back toward the front entrance, then in
through the glass doors. A young girl wearing the brown
smock many of the hourly staffers wore greeted her at the
desk. "How can I help you today?"

Rhonda noticed her name tag. "Hi, Marie. My name is
Rhonda. A few days ago I attended the orientation class and
signed up to be a dog walker. So, this is my first official day
as a volunteer. My friend Connie was supposed to be here,
but she's not feeling well. I decided to be brave and come on
my own."

"Well, we're glad you did. And congrats on this being
your first day. Do you know where you're going, who to talk
to?"

"Not completely. Connie said I should mention, because
of a health issue, I can only walk smaller dogs."

"That's not a problem," Marie said. "Our smaller dogs

will appreciate the attention. Do you know where our kennel is for the smaller dogs?"

Rhonda shook her head no. "But if you point my nose in the right direction, I'll find it."

"Okay, just go directly through that door behind me, you'll see a big hallway. Walk to the end, through a door on your right. Ask for Angela, if you don't see her. She should be wearing a smock like mine. Just tell her what you told me, and she should get you all set."

"Thank you very much." *See, that wasn't so hard.*

She signed in on the clipboard, then followed Marie's instructions. But when she opened the door, she didn't see Angela. In fact, there were no humans inside. But no doubt, she was in the right place. About fifteen small dogs all greeted her at the same time. The sound was almost deafening. Two of the walls were lined with two layers of cages. About half of them were filled with dogs. Along the other two walls were bigger pens, the kind you'd expect to see occupied by a big dog. But she noticed these were all completely filled, and all had one dog each. As she studied the scene further, she realized the dogs in the double-decker cages were all very small, like Chihuahuas and Yorkie-sized dogs. The ones in the bigger pens were still small, but seemed to be about knee-high. About the size her Amos had been.

All the dogs were trying to get her attention, as if to say, "Pick me, pick me." She looked back at the door, wondering if she should go looking for Angela. But curiosity got the better of her, so she began reading the little cards tucked inside of sleeves attached to each cage. On them was all the information the shelter had on the dog in each pen.

So much of what she read tugged at her heart. So many little dog stories. She'd have to be careful. Couldn't let herself get attached here. She had a job to do. She reminded herself she was here to help get these dogs ready for other people to adopt. But she also realized, it would be impossible for her to decide which one to walk first. They were all so eager as they vied for her attention.

That is, all except one.

In the bigger pens, all the dogs except one were right there at the door, pleading for her to pick them. But not the dog in the right-hand corner of the room. For a moment, she thought the pen might be empty until she stepped closer and saw it had a sleeve with doggy information card inside. Another few steps and she saw a little, long-haired mostly-black dog all curled up in a dog bed at the back of the pen. There were a few dog toys in a pile on one side and a food and water bowl on the other. Both were full and neither looked like they'd been touched.

She wondered if the dog was asleep, but saw its eyes were open. The dog was staring at the back corner of the pen, totally disinterested in her presence. And that's what caught Rhonda's attention the most. Every other dog in the room was doing anything they could to get her to look their way, and here was one dog who seemed to be sending a message to *please leave me alone.*

Was it deaf? Maybe that was it. Rhonda pulled the info card out of its sleeve and saw the name in capital letters: "BAILEY." Next to that, the box for Female was checked.

"Bailey," she called out, gently. But no reaction. She said it again. Still gently but a little louder. Nothing. "Bailey," she said at a volume loud enough to be heard over all the barking dogs. That got a slight reaction. Bailey looked up at Rhonda, but only for a moment then returned to her position.

But Rhonda saw something in that moment. In those eyes.

She wasn't deaf. She was...sad. Extremely sad.

"You poor thing," Rhonda said.

8

BAILEY COULD HEAR THE NICE WOMAN STANDING OUTSIDE HER
cage. She could tell she was nice, not just by the way she
talked but her mood. But she wasn't interested in company.
The only familiar thing in this totally strange place was her
bed, and the dark checkered blanket she was laying on.
They still had the smells of home. But nothing else did. And
she didn't recognize anyone. A few times that nice woman
she met the first day had come by, the one who talked with
Bill, the one who kept petting her after Bill left. She had
been okay with that until it became clear Bill was not
returning.

And Harold did not come back, either.

She felt certain that one of them would. But so much
time had gone by, more time than she'd ever been away
from Harold. He would leave her for a while at the house
sometimes by herself. But he always came back.

Always.

So much so, she never worried that he would leave and never return. He always came back. When he did, he would be so happy to see her. But nowhere near as happy as she was to see him. And then he might not leave again for many days. She liked those days the best, when he stayed home.

But now he was gone. And she didn't know why. She didn't know how long it had been since she'd seen him last. And she was starting to believe she might never see him again.

And that thought made her so terribly sad.

RHONDA SQUATTED down in front of Bailey's cage and continued to gently talk to her, hoping to get Bailey to look at her again. For some reason, this became the urgent task, not walking one of the many dogs eager for her attention.

Just then the door opened. She turned to see Kim Harper come in with a younger girl wearing a brown smock. Rhonda stood to greet them and saw the girl's name tag. It was Angela.

Both looked at Rhonda.

"I remember you," Kim said. "From our orientation class the other day."

Rhonda walked toward her extending her hand. "You're right. My name's Rhonda. I signed up to be one of the dog walkers. This is my first official day, in fact."

"Well, glad you're here," Kim said.

"The other young lady at the front desk — I forget her name just now — told me to come back here and see

Angela, since I'm interested in walking smaller dogs. Well, it's actually because of my hip. I think big dogs are fine."

"Well, I'm Angela. And our small dogs would love to get to know you better. I see you were over there by Bailey's pen when we came in. Don't think she's quite up for a walk just yet. Wish she was. Actually at this point, I'd be happy if she would just look at me. That's why I went to get Kim. See if she had any ideas. See if there's anything I'm doing wrong."

"I saw on her little card there," Rhonda said, "that she's only been here a few days. Has she been like that the whole time?"

"Pretty much," Angela said. "Every time I've been here."

"Is that normal?" Rhonda said. "I mean, I can see why any dog would be depressed if their owner just left them here. But for that many days? All the other dogs seem totally over it."

Kim took a few steps toward Bailey's pen. "I am a little concerned for how depressed she is, and for how long she's been like this. You're right, though, all dogs struggle at first. Who can blame them? We have no way of explaining to them what's happened. Bailey has some other factors in play, though. She's eleven, and she had been with her owner the entire time, since she was a puppy. And from my understanding, for that entire time he was retired. So they were pretty much together 24/7. So, we're talking a deep, embedded level of bonding there."

"Well," Rhonda said. "Guess that explains it." She looked back at Bailey and felt even more compassion for her. It was probably the equivalent of when Rhonda had lost Ted suddenly after so many years together. Only imagine how much more her grief would have been compounded had Ted just suddenly disappeared without any explanation whatsoever?

"Can you think of anything I could be doing for her?" Angela asked Kim.

"Not really. I'm hoping in a day or so she'll start to respond better, start to pull out of it. Her chances of being re-homed are extremely challenging, as it is."

"You mean because of her age?" Rhonda said.

"That's certainly part of it," Kim said. "But in Bailey's case, she's got a few other strikes against her. I don't know how much you read on her card..."

"Just the first few lines," Rhonda said.

"Well, besides being eleven, she's not good with children or with other dogs."

"Oh. Does she bite?" said Rhonda.

"No, nothing like that. They said she's never shown any signs of aggression toward anyone. She's just incredibly shy. Her owner wrote a note saying she used to love kids when she was younger, but then his grandkids stopped coming over for a long period of time. Dogs do that sometimes. Some dogs, anyway. They get out of practice with children, and then kids can be pretty unpredictable, which doesn't help. At least from a dog's perspective. Chasing after them, always wanting to pick them up. Especially small dogs. They treat them like they're a puppy when they'd rather be left alone. Since that's how Bailey is, it eliminates one more big block of people willing to consider adopting her. Anyone with small children, or even grandparents with small grandchildren. And anyone who has another dog or cat."

No one said anything for a moment. They all just stood there looking at Bailey. Rhonda realized, during this entire conversation Bailey's name came up several times. But Bailey didn't look up, not even once. Her Amos? He ever heard her or Ted talking about him, his ears perked right up, like he was trying to decipher every word. Then Rhonda remembered something she'd seen on a video from an online dog group that rescued strays. "Say, Kim, can I run something by you?"

"You mean about Bailey?"

"Yes, just an idea. You may already know about it..."

"What is it?" Kim said.

"I saw a video online once about this dog that had been living on its own for a long time. This group rescued it from this rundown part of town and brought it to their shelter. It had way more problems than Bailey does. Its coat was a mess, it was malnourished. But it acted the same way Bailey does around people. Just completely aloof and disinterested. Would even look away from them the way she does. On the video, this one guy started spending time in this dog's pen, just to create some sense of connection. He wouldn't bother the dog, just stay on the front end of the gate but inside it, so there was no physical barrier between them. He'd talk gently to the dog but didn't make any attempts to force the dog to interact with him. After a while he was able to feed it, then pet it, then eventually it started coming over to him."

"I've seen videos like that," Kim said. "If you're asking if I'm okay with you trying that, the answer is yes."

"I mean," Rhonda said, "I'd be doing that instead of walking one of these dogs."

"I understand," Kim said. "We have lots of volunteers willing to walk dogs. If you get tired of just sitting there, you could try reading to her. Believe it or not, dogs like being read to."

Rhonda smiled. "And you're sure she won't bite."

"I never say never, when it comes to dogs," Kim said. "But especially if you do what you just described, waiting on her to come to you, I can't imagine why she would try to hurt you. Her owner described her as the sweetest thing on earth."

Rhonda walked over to Bailey's pen and squatted down. "Then I think I'd like to give it a try."

9

OFFICER NED BARRINGTON HURRIED HOME AND PULLED INTO his usual space at the Bent Oak Apartments. He had just taken a half-day's personal leave for a very important mission. He trotted up the outside stairway and rounded the corner leading to his front door. He was surprised to see Russell standing there, unlocking his door. Russell was Ned's next door neighbor, a sixth-grader at the local middle school.

"I forgot you were coming over today," Ned said. He looked at his watch. "School let out early?"

Russell looked up at him as the deadbolt unlatched. "No, I'm playing hooky. But don't tell anyone, especially the cops."

"Very funny." Ned enjoyed Russell's sense of humor.

"We didn't have school today. Teacher workday, whatever that means. As opposed to the teacher-teach-days, I guess. When they work, we get off. So, I thought I'd let

Parker out. Didn't know you'd be coming home. Don't you usually work for a few more hours?"

"Yeah," Ned said, "but I took the rest of the shift off."

Russell pulled the key out of the lock. "Well, since you're here, guess you can let Parker out."

"Actually, if you don't mind, there's something I'd like to do. I was just coming home for a quick change and to take care of him. How about you still let him out, maybe take him for a walk, and I'll pay you extra this week?"

"Works for me," Russell said. "Almost feel guilty you paying me to do this. Me and Parker are good buds. Hardly feels like work."

Just then they both heard Parker whining and barking on the other side of the door. Russell opened it, gave Parker the "Place" command. Something Kim had taught Parker to do when someone comes to the door. Parker would go to a fixed spot in the foyer and wait there until he was released. Kept him from darting out through the open door and gave people a chance to get in without being assaulted by an excited small dog.

Ned always got a kick out of seeing Parker sit there like that, as if held by some invisible chain. He wanted so badly to greet him and Russell, his whole body was vibrating. Once the door was closed, Russell said, "Release." Parker ran to Russell, then over to Ned, then back to Russell, then back to Ned. His whole back and tail wagging.

"Who's a good boy?" Russell said, bending down to pet Parker and rub him all over. "You miss me, boy?"

"Obviously, he did," Ned said. Parker was paying twice as

much attention to him. "Can you take care of him while I go get changed?"

"I sure will," Russell said, more to Parker. "I'll bet somebody's got to go out. Don't you, boy? You been holding it all day. Let's go get that leash." Parker ran to where his leash was hanging on a hook.

Ned headed back into his bedroom to change. He heard the front door open and close. It was so nice to have Russell next door. He didn't mind the little bit of money he paid him. Because of Russell's love for the dog, he put a lot of his own time in off the clock. Like here, Russell had come over on his own. Had Ned not come home, he'd have never known about it.

Up until a month ago, Ned had been paying Russell on something of a barter system. Ned paid for Russell's martial arts classes in exchange for the dog-watching. But the dojo had shut down for some major plumbing repairs. That was another thing Ned liked about Russell. The way he dug into these self-defense lessons. Ned had wondered if Russell would let it go once the bullying situation at his school had ended.

But he'd stuck with it. And it was clear, the experience had done a number on Russell's whole outlook. He wasn't that nervous, timid youngster with a black eye Ned had met some months ago. He was a confident young man, who now actually enjoyed going to school. And it seemed to Ned that Russell had actually put on some weight recently. The good kind.

Just as Ned finished getting dressed, he heard the front door open and close again. "What a good boy you were,"

Russell said. "You didn't even bark at that other dog. And he was being so rude."

Ned came out into the living area, watched Parker following Russell around. When he saw Ned, Parker ran over to him and jumped up on the couch, then onto the back of the couch to get as close to Ned as he could. "That's my boy." Ned gave him a hug and held him close for a moment. "Have some trouble on the walk?"

"No, not with this guy." Russell pointed to Parker. "Across the street, there was this big Shepherd mix pitching a fit because Parker was on the earth. Parker starts lunging for him — as if he had a prayer against this thug — and I give him the *Ignore* command, and he instantly stops. He looks up at me, like he's apologizing, and starts walking right beside like he's supposed to. The whole time, until we turn the corner, you can hear that Shepherd screaming and swearing at Parker, and his owner screaming and swearing at him to stop."

Ned laughed.

"I'm telling you, Kim really knows her stuff. Ever since you and her been together, and she started training Parker, he's like a different dog. Still got all his personality, but he's so obedient."

"She really is amazing," Ned said. "In fact, her being amazing is why I took the rest of the day off."

"You two going out?"

"No. Actually, I didn't tell her I was doing this. And if she asks, you never saw me come home."

Russell gave him a puzzled look. "For starters, Kim never

contacts me regarding your whereabouts, so don't think that's gonna be a problem. But why all the secrecy?"

"How good are you at keeping secrets?"

Russell shoots Ned his wiseguy look. "I could work for the CIA." He gets a thought. "Back in the day when they didn't leak like a sieve."

This kid. Ned walked behind the couch over to the hutch by the front door to get his keys. "I'm going to go see my mother."

"This...is your secret?"

Ned laughed. "To ask her for a ring. And not just any ring. My grandmother's engagement ring."

Russell's eyes bugged out. "You gonna pop the question?"

Ned nodded. "Pretty soon. First, I gotta see if any of my other siblings have dibs on this ring. If so, I'm gonna have to order one. If not, and my mom's okay with it, then yeah. I'll be popping the question pretty soon."

"Well, it's about time," Russell said. "Me and my mom were talking about that at dinner a few nights ago. When's this Ned gonna ask her? my mom says. I said, I know, right? Never met two people more obviously meant to be together."

Ned smiled. The brain on this kid. They could be friends, good friends, if he were just a little older. "Well, thanks, Russell. Nice to hear you say that. So, you think she'll say yes?"

An incredulous look came over Russell's face. "Before you finish getting done your spiel. So, don't bother making it a long one."

10

On the way home from the Humane Society, Rhonda stopped off at a local family-owned grocery store that specialized in great produce. Connie had texted her saying she had a hankering for grapes and wondered if Rhonda could pick some up for her. Rhonda decided to grab a few things for herself, as well. And it would give her a few moments to reenter normal life, doing normal things. Like shopping.

Not like sitting in a dog pen on a small chair with a depressed dog for ninety minutes.

Kim had suggested she should talk gently to Bailey, but she shouldn't make any physical moves toward her. Like trying to pet her. Again, not that she would bite Rhonda. But the idea was to let Bailey make the first move. The only problem was, it didn't happen. Bailey never made any moves in Rhonda's direction. Only at the very end, a few minutes before Rhonda had to leave, did she even seem to acknowledge Rhonda's presence. Nothing so dramatic as a tail-wagging, but she did lift her head briefly and look at Rhonda.

But she didn't have a dog smile on her face. More like an expression that said, *Why are you still here*? Then she'd rested her chin back on her front paws, as before.

Kim had checked in with her before Rhonda left. After hearing Rhonda's update, she thanked her for her patience and said she wasn't that surprised to hear how things went. Some dogs are great with people but some mostly bond to one person their whole life, Kim had explained. Bailey must be the latter. And she had bonded to her owner for eleven years, since her first memories as a pup.

Kim said Rhonda could expect it to take a few more similar sessions before Bailey began to show any signs of improvement. But she'd also quickly added that Rhonda didn't have to continue with this little project. She'd perfectly understand if Rhonda wanted to let it go and walk regular dogs as she'd originally intended.

Rhonda thought about all these things again as she rolled her cart through the store, through the checkout line, and on the drive home. She was still wrestling with it when she walked into Connie's place with her bag of grapes. She rinsed the grapes off in the sink and put them in a ziplock bag. "Are you still back in the bedroom?" she yelled down the hall.

"I am," Connie said. "You got my grapes?"

"I've got your grapes." She brought them into the bedroom, stood by the doorway. Didn't look like Connie had moved much since she last saw her. "You look a little better. How are you feeling?"

"About the same. Not sneezing anymore, so that's some progress. You could just toss that bag here if you don't want to get too close."

Rhonda had just thought the same thing. "I really don't want to get sick." She tossed the bag on the bed.

"I don't know why I'm craving these so much, but I've really been waiting for you to get back with them. I heard you rinsing them off. Appreciate that. Want to have a few before I get my cooties on them?"

Rhonda laughed. "No, thanks. I'm craving a turkey and Swiss sandwich."

"How much I owe you for the grapes?"

"My treat. They almost give them away at that place anyhow. Prices are so cheap."

"I know it. I kept thinking after they opened last year, they were just that low to get people coming in. But they've stayed that low ever since."

"Well," Rhonda said, "I better get next door. Don't want to keep my stomach waiting too much longer on that sandwich."

"Thanks again for the grapes," Connie said. "Before you go, you didn't tell me how your first day at the shelter went?"

"Oh, guess I didn't."

"That doesn't sound too good. Something go wrong?"

"Not exactly wrong. More like...confusing."

"Really?" Connie said. "Don't think I've ever had a confusing day down there. You got my curiosity up."

Rhonda went on to explain the whole situation with Bailey, including how things ended up and what Kim had said.

"Okay, I'd say that qualifies as confusing. Do you think you made a mistake? There's so many other dogs down there that would love to have that kind of attention."

"I know. I thought about that. But now that I know her situation, I don't feel right giving up on her so quickly. It's not like she's choosing to be difficult. And she certainly didn't bring this situation down on herself. She was just living her life being this great little dog, and then one day for a reason no one can explain to her, she gets dropped off in this strange place all alone. Think if that happened to me, I'd be doing just as bad. But the problem is, if she can't snap out of it, no one will ever adopt her."

"Yeah," Connie said, "that's a tough one. Don't know what to tell you. Maybe you should just give it some time, think about it some more. I'll pray God gives you some wisdom, too."

"Thanks. I'm not scheduled to go back till the day after tomorrow. Hopefully, I'll have a better handle on what I'm supposed to do."

11

NED PULLED INTO THE FAMILIAR DRIVEWAY OF HIS BOYHOOD home. It's where his parents still lived. They bought it new back in 1985, spent the last five years updating everything. But none of the changes had erased or even diminished the myriad of memories made here. Most of them positive. His parents weren't perfect, by any means. But he'd lived long enough and had heard enough negative family memories shared by friends to know he and his siblings had gotten a pretty good deal.

His parents were both retired and had been empty-nesters for quite a few years, but Ned's father couldn't quite bring himself to sell the family homestead or trade it in for something newer or smaller. That's what his mother preferred. She had joked there was plenty of time to do that after he kicked the bucket. Ned got out of his car and walked past the well-manicured sidewalk toward the front door. He smiled recalling how much better the yard looked now since the days he and his little brother argued about whose turn it was to mow. Of course, who knows how nice it would have looked then had his father been willing to pay them what he'd dished out every month to these lawn guys.

Ned knocked once then opened the door. "It's me, Mom." He'd called first, so he knew she was home. His dad was at the shop getting a new set of tires put on the car. Which was fine. This was a conversation he felt better having with his mom.

"I'm in the kitchen, Ned, starting on dinner."

He walked through the foyer and the living area, immaculate as always, and into the kitchen. This was the most recently renovated room in the house. "Isn't it a little early for dinner?"

"Trying a new recipe," she said, "for a pot roast. They take hours to do 'em right. We had this at a friend's house a few weeks ago, and your father went on and on about it for days. So, I got the recipe and decided to surprise him with it. Have a feeling he'll know what it is by the smell whenever he gets back from his errands."

Ned took a strong sniff. "I don't smell anything different."

"Haven't started cooking it yet, silly. But you wait. An hour or two from now? This whole place is gonna smell amazing. You're welcome to stay for dinner if you don't have any plans."

"I just might." He came behind her and gave her a peck on the cheek.

"Glad you came over," she said. "This your day off?"

"No, actually took some personal leave time. Pretty

much just to come talk with you. Wanted to do this in person."

"Uh-oh. Is something wrong?" She walked over to the sink, washed her hands then picked up a towel.

"No, nothing's wrong. It's something positive. Just not the kind of thing I wanted to do over the phone."

She put the dish towel back on the rack. "Is this going to take long? It's okay if it is, but I should probably get this pot roast a little further along."

"Shouldn't take long," Ned said. "A few minutes, is all."

"Then let's go sit in the living room. If you came all this way just talk to me, least I can do is give you my full attention."

They headed into the living room, his mother went for her favorite chair. He sat on the couch close to her.

"So, what's going on? Don't take too long to get to the headline."

Ned hated when she said things like that. He was all about setting up the main point with a good story. Maybe he could find some kind of compromise here. "You know Kim and I have been seeing each other for several months now."

"And we like Kim, your father and I. Wish she was around when we had dogs."

"Yeah, she's like a wizard with dogs. You can't believe the difference with Parker, since she trained him."

"He's such a cute little guy. I mean, now. So glad his hair all came back."

"Yeah, he's definitely my buddy. Anyway, I haven't talked about this too much, about how I feel about Kim."

"No, you haven't. But it's pretty obvious you're nuts about

her. Your father and I can both tell...we've never seen you behave this way toward any of the girlfriends you had. Not that you had that many, but you're clearly more attracted to her than any of the others."

"Well, here's a headline for you. I'm not just attracted to Kim. I love her, Mom. She's the one."

His mother was clearly taken aback by that. "Well, that's..." Tears welled up in her eyes. "That's getting it out there. Very good, son. I think we knew that, but now we don't have to be guessing about it. Your sister, Jean, said she thought you were in love. She likes Kim, too."

Ned got up and got a tissue from a box on the hutch, brought it back to his mom. "No, there's no guesswork for me. I've pretty much felt like this from the very beginning. Then you know we had that little...*bump*, right after I got shot during that bank robbery."

His mom sighed. "Don't need to be reminded about that. One of the worst days of my life."

"You know I'm fine now, right? I hardly ever even think about it anymore."

"I know, just go on with what you were saying. Talking about that bump you and Kim had in the beginning. I remember that, too."

"Well, after she came around again, and ever since, I haven't had a moment's doubt about her. I've just been taking it slow and easy, because, well, I'm not a kid anymore. The stakes get a bit higher in these matters. Just wanted to give it enough time to make sure there weren't going to be any surprises that might shut this thing down, for her or for me."

"I take it, there haven't been any? About now, I could use another headline."

Ned laughed. "No, no surprises. I'm pretty sure she feels the same about me. If I'm wrong, then I'm in serious trouble."

"I don't think you're wrong," his mother said. "So..."

"So, I'm going to ask her to marry me."

His mother smiled. It was a nice smile. But it wasn't quite the overjoyed reaction Ned expected.

"I thought that's where this was heading," she said.

"Okay, but aren't you happy for me? Isn't this the kind of news a mother usually gets excited about?"

"I am...happy for you. Really, Ned, I am. It's just...I don't know. How sure are you that she's okay with what you...with your chosen profession, I guess we could say?"

"She's totally fine with it."

"That's good. I'm not trying to be difficult. But you said it yourself, in the beginning there was this...bump. As I recall, she ended the relationship, because she didn't think she could live being a cop's wife. I wasn't mad at her when I heard about it, though I was hurting for you. But it's not for everyone. You know that. Look at how many of your policeman friends have had difficult marriages, how many of them didn't make it. I guess I just want to make sure you and Kim have settled that part of it. That she's really prepared for the kind of life she'd be signing up for."

Hearing this helped Ned calm down. "Okay, is that your only hesitation to this news? If this wasn't a thing..."

"Then I'd be as excited as any other mother finding out her son is getting married to a wonderful girl."

"Then," Ned said, "you can start getting excited. Kim and I have talked this out. I'd say thoroughly. You know she's a believer, like us. She would say God has put faith in her heart for this. Meaning, being with me. Although, we didn't specifically talk about marriage, but that was kind of on the table. But there's also this, Mom. She means more to me than being a cop. If we're not seeing things clearly, and my job does become a major snag in our marriage...well, it's just a job. I'll find something else to do."

The tears returned in his mother's eyes. She reached over to give him a hug. "Okay," she said during the hug, "I'm officially excited now."

After the hug, Ned said, "There's one more headline, I guess you could say. More a favor, or a question. I was thinking about giving Kim Grandma's engagement ring, if you and Dad are okay with it, and if none of the other siblings have dibs on it."

"Well," she said, "considering that your older sister is already married, and Jean...well, when she gets to that point, it's not customary for the groom to ask the bride's family if they have any family heirlooms available. And your little brother isn't even serious about anyone. And even if he was..."

"There's gotta be some privileges being the older brother." Ned laughed.

"It's fine with me," she said. "And I can pretty much tell you what your father would say."

"What's that?"

"*We kept that old ring?*"

Ned laughed some more. "I can see that. So, I can use it?"

"It's all yours, son. I can't wait to hear how it goes when you ask her. When's that gonna be? Do you know?"

"Well, now that I know I can use Grandma's ring, I'll get right on the *when* part."

12

Summerville Humane Society
Following Morning

WHEN BAILEY AWOKE, SHE SADLY DISCOVERED SHE WAS BACK in this horrible place. She had been having the nicest dream. She was back home where she belonged, the place where everything made sense. Of course, Harold was there and they were going through their normal morning routines together. She had been walking the usual route she'd take through her large fenced-in backyard, making sure no squirrels were about. Checking the tops of the fences especially. That's where they liked to sneak around. For some reason, she didn't hear them as well as she used to, but she could certainly see them.

But today — in her dream — the fences were clear.

Every ten steps or so, she'd pause and look at Harold, just in case he had been trying to call her in. But there he was on the brick patio, sitting in his usual chair reading the same book he read every morning. Occasionally taking sips from the same mug he always drank from. It wasn't as hot outside as some mornings, and a nice breeze was blowing the palm trees around.

Everything was as it should be.

When she'd made one pass through the entire backyard, she began going back the other way. Before she reached the first corner she thought she heard Harold calling her. She looked his way. He was standing, waving for her to come. She ran toward him as fast as she could, but when she got there he disappeared. She looked all over for him, first on the patio then in the backyard. But he was nowhere to be found.

That's when she woke up and found herself here. In this awful place once again.

All alone.

RHONDA PULLED into the shelter parking lot. She had signed up to come two to three times a week, and she had just been there yesterday, but she couldn't stop thinking about that poor little dog. When she had filled out the volunteer form, the coordinator gal had said she could put down as many times as she could come in a week. They needed all the help they could get, so Rhonda knew no one would complain about her coming back again today.

She locked her purse in the trunk and headed inside. A

different girl manned the reception desk. Once Rhonda explained who she was and why she was there, she happily let her sign in. "You know where to go?" she asked.

"I do," Rhonda said. "Was just here yesterday. Do you know if Angela is still working with the small dogs today?"

"I believe she is."

Rhonda smiled and made her way through the hallways to the small dog kennel area. When she came in, this time Angela was there. Looked like she was changing the dogs' water bowls. Of course, all the dogs were on their feet straining to catch a glimpse of Angela through their cages. The ones right in front of her were pitching a happy fit.

"I'll get to you next," Angela said to the chihuahua in the cage next to the one she was working in. "Everybody's going to get some."

The dogs in the front half of the room shifted their attention to Rhonda, started making all kinds of fuss like they did yesterday.

"Oh, hi," Angela said over her shoulder. "I'm sorry, I forgot your name."

"It's Rhonda. I was here yesterday afternoon."

"I do remember that. And now that you say it, I remember your name. Well, let's hope I will for the next time. I'm better with faces than names."

Rhonda glanced over at Bailey's pen. Not surprisingly, she was once again the only dog not trying to get either hers or Angela's attention. She was still laying in the back all curled up, head resting on her front paws. She was, however, lying on the opposite side today.

"Let me guess," Angela said, "you're here for Bailey again. A real sucker for punishment, eh?"

"I suppose. I notice she's laying in the opposite corner this morning. I guess that's proof she can move."

Angela laughed. "I've seen her move, once or twice. She'll get up to drink a little bit, but then go right back to the same place."

"She doesn't eat?"

"Not so I can tell. Hope she snaps out of it soon, or we might have to get the vet involved. Can't have a dog starving herself to death."

"What about her going the bathroom? I don't see any messes. It didn't smell bad when I was in there yesterday."

"See that little dog flap in the corner?" Angela said. "That leads to a pen about the same size on the outside. Normally, the dogs will go when we take them for a walk. But since she's not in the mood for walking, we're letting her do her business in the outside pen. I've cleaned it up a couple of times, but she's not going much since she's not eating much. Feel free to put that chair in there like you did yesterday. I can get you something to read to her. Unless you want to walk one of these other dogs instead."

"No, I'm here for Bailey. Don't know if I can make a difference but feels like I've gotta try."

Rhonda walked over and picked up the chair that she used yesterday, brought it to Bailey's pen. "Hey there, girl. Remember me?" she said the kindest way she knew how. "Thought I'd come for another visit."

She opened the gate as quietly as she could. Considering all the noise the other dogs were making, it likely didn't matter. She set the chair down on the opposite side from yesterday, so that she was facing the dog. Bailey looked at her briefly, without lifting her head, then looked away.

"I see you in there," she said. "I know you're very sad, and I understand why. Wish there was some way to explain to you what's going on. All I can do is try to be here for you, help you see other people can be perfectly safe to be around."

"You're a dog talker like me," Angela said. "People tell me I'm an idiot for doing it, say they don't know 95% of the words you're saying. Maybe they're right, but their eyes tell me they're getting a whole lot more than that."

"I always talked to my dogs," Rhonda said. "Might've been more for me than them, but I'm like you, I think they get more than people give them credit for. Maybe they read the way we're saying the words, not just the words themselves." She looked down at Bailey. "That it, girl? Can you tell I'm just trying to help you?"

Bailey looked up at her again, just briefly, and just the eyes. But to Rhonda, it was something. She looked around and saw a big pillow on a shelf. "Say, Angela? Could I trade out this chair for that pillow over there? Maybe if I get closer to the ground it might help."

"Sure. That's what I use it for."

"Won't need any help sitting down on it," Rhonda said, "but might need your help getting back up."

"You go right ahead."

Rhonda got up slowly and left the pen, taking the chair with her. She put it back in its place and reached for the pillow. As she came back, she held it out in front of Bailey's cage. "See, girl? Just a pillow. Not gonna hurt you any." She went back inside, set the pillow down where the chair had been and used the chain-link fence to help lower herself onto the pillow. That got a reaction from Bailey. Her eyes opened wide, and she lifted her head slightly.

"It's okay, Bailey," Rhonda said in a soothing voice. "Just wanted to get a little closer to you, that's all."

Then Bailey did something disturbing.

Was she growling at Rhonda? She didn't hear anything, but Bailey was certainly showing her teeth. She lifted her head, looked at Rhonda and did it again. "Angela, could you come over here for a moment and look at Bailey?"

"Something wrong?"

"I think so," Rhonda said. "Guess she doesn't like me getting closer. She's showing her teeth at me. What should I do?"

Angela came over and looked down. "Yeah, that doesn't look good. Maybe you should come on out of there. Do you need my help?"

"I'm not sure." Maybe it was the adrenaline rush, but Rhonda was able to lift herself up pulling against the openings in the chain-link. Angela slid the gate open as Rhonda slipped out. They both looked down at Bailey.

She had lowered her head once again to where it was before, looking away, resting it on her front paws.

"I better go get Kim," Angela said, "let her know what just happened. She's gonna want to know that Bailey's showing signs of aggression."

13

Kim was just finishing up an assessment of a newly surrendered dog, one of the many hats she wore as the Animal Behavior Manager. After dogs had been surrendered by owners and processed through the Intake area, it was her job to evaluate them on a couple of different levels. The first, of course, was the area of aggression. Obviously, the shelter couldn't release dangerous dogs into the general public. That is, of course, unless they were small. For some reason, lots of would-be dog owners didn't mind aggressive dogs if they were small and cute.

Some even found the trait to be almost endearing. Still, even with small dogs, she had to evaluate their level of aggression to properly warn small dog lovers on what they could expect from a particular dog.

Another area of evaluation was a dog's temperament. Was it playful or more relaxed? Was it energetic and needed a big yard, or was it more of a lapdog totally suited for an apartment or condo? Was it more of a one-owner type or a better fit for a family with kids?

"So, how did this new fellow do?" Sabrina said. She was working at the Intake desk today and had brought the dog being evaluated to Kim.

Kim sat down and gave the black and white spotted spaniel mix a hug. "This guy passed with flying colors, didn't you boy?" His tail wagged, and he licked Kim's hand. "Not an aggressive bone in his body. And as you can see, pretty much loves everybody. My guess is someone will put a hold on him within a couple of hours after he gets on the adoption floor." She handed Sabrina the filled-out form, so she could create the official card that would go into the dog's sleeve.

Just then the door opened. Angela came in looking almost upset.

"Kim, is there any chance you could come to my area? Like, right now?"

"Sure, Angela. I'm done here for the moment. What's wrong?"

"It's Bailey. You know, the small dog in my area who's totally shut down?"

"I remember. What's going on?"

"Well, hate to say it, but she's coming out of it a little, but not in a good way."

"What do you mean?"

"Let's head over there." Angela walked back into the hallway. Kim followed. "That lady, Rhonda, the new volunteer who came yesterday and just sat with her instead of walking other dogs? Well, she came back again this morning. She said she kept thinking about Bailey ever since she left and wanted to come back to see if she could help her."

"And what happened?" Kim said.

"At first, nothing. Just like yesterday. But then Rhonda got an idea. She saw those floor pillows I sometimes use when I want to get close to one of the dogs and asked if she could try that with Bailey, instead of the chair. I didn't see any harm in it, since you didn't think Bailey had any aggression issues."

"That's right. I don't have a problem with that. Why? Did Bailey react to it?"

"Afraid so. She growled at Rhonda, showed her teeth. Rhonda got scared, and I had to hurry over there and let her out."

"Really? She growled at Rhonda?"

"Think so. Think that's what Rhonda said." The door was just up ahead on the right. "As soon as Rhonda got out of there, Bailey went right back to her shutdown position. You know, curled up in the back, looking away."

Kim could hardly believe what she was hearing. According to the owners, Bailey had never shown any signs of aggression, and she had passed Kim's aggression test easily, even in her shutdown condition. She thought she knew what it might be, but didn't say anything until she could see Bailey for herself.

Kim walked in and, of course, all the dogs pitched a fit. Most of them by now recognized Kim. All except Bailey, who was still curled up in her pen. Rhonda was standing nearby leaning on a set of shelves, looking at Bailey from a distance. She turned when she heard the commotion.

"Hi, Kim. I'm Rhonda Hawthorne. I was here—"

"I remember you, Rhonda. Thanks for coming back." She extended her hand and Rhonda shook it.

"Maybe it was a mistake," Rhonda said looking discouraged.

Kim glanced at Bailey. Just seeing her all but confirmed what she had suspected. "I don't think it was," she said. She walked up to Bailey's pen, pulled the card out of the sleeve. Bailey looked up at her for a moment, eyes only. Kim read the info in the block about "Breed." She turned to Rhonda. "Did Bailey actually growl at you?"

Rhonda thought a moment. "No, she didn't make a sound. And I still hear pretty well."

"I'm sorry," Angela said. "Guess I heard you wrong."

"Tell me exactly what happened," said Kim. "You were sitting in a chair at first, right?"

"Yes, like yesterday. But then I saw that pillow and wondered if it might not help if I could get closer to the ground. So very calmly, I switched them out then slowly sat down on the pillow. I started talking to Bailey in a soothing tone of voice."

"Did you try to pet her?"

"No. Just words, like yesterday. And the next thing I know, she lifts her head and shows me her teeth. It was pretty shocking. Pretty much the opposite reaction I was hoping for."

Kim smiled. She was sure of it now.

"I don't get why you're smiling?" Angela said. "Doesn't that bother you?"

"No," Kim said. "Not at all. As a matter fact, Rhonda, this

isn't an opposite reaction to the one you were hoping for. For Bailey, I would call it a significant step forward."

The looks on both Rhonda's and Angela's faces could not have been more puzzled.

Kim held up Bailey's info card. "See, in the section on her breed it says, *mini-Aussie mix.* I'd say in Bailey's case, she's more of a toy than a mini. And judging by her looks and especially this unusual display you both experienced, I'd say Bailey is *mostly* an Aussie, if not completely. I don't think she's a mix."

"I don't understand," Rhonda said.

"Me, either," Angela said. "For starters, what's the difference between a mini and a toy?"

"The difference is just one of size," Kim said. "Mini-Australian shepherds were bred from full-sized Aussies. Some say breeders kept breeding the runts until genetically, they started producing Aussies that were just smaller. And it worked. A new, smaller breed of Aussies was created. They were every bit the same as full-sized versions, just smaller. Then it appears — although I'm not totally sure — the same thing was done with mini-Aussies to create a toy version. They aren't as tiny as, say, Pomeranian's or Chihuahuas. More like...Bailey's size. So, you've got full-sized Aussies, minis...about a third smaller, and toy Aussies who only weigh about fifteen to twenty pounds. As a matter fact, I think I'll change her card right now." Kim crossed through the word *mini* and wrote the word *toy* above it. Then crossed out the word *mix.*

"What about her showing her teeth?" Rhonda asked.

"That, my friend, is something Aussies are known for. It's called the *Aussie Grin*."

"Grin?" Angela repeated. "You mean Bailey was smiling at Rhonda?"

Kim smiled. "In a way, yes. The Aussie Grin has a few other layers, but none of them have anything to do with aggression. When Aussies get nervous, sometimes when they're excited, and sometimes when they're very happy... this grin appears on their face. Of course, to most people, it looks like what both of you thought. But that's not what's going on with Bailey, at all. She wasn't mad or angry with you."

Rhonda almost smiled. "That's a relief. Are you saying she was happy with me? Was this like...making some progress?"

"Not sure we can say she was happy with you. Remember, I said they also do it when they're nervous? My guess would be, it was that. You were coming closer, by sitting down near the floor next to her, and she was feeling a little nervous about it, so she grinned."

"Was she telling me—politely—to back off?"

"Maybe, but I don't think so. Maybe more like...take it slow. Let's not move too fast here. Something like that. But it's still a positive step. She's starting to communicate, which she hasn't been willing to do before."

"What do you suggest we do now?"

"I'd say, let's try it again while I stand back here and watch."

14

Kim, Angela, and Rhonda were all facing Bailey's pen. Rhonda stepped forward and was just about to open the gate when the main door opened. They turned to see a woman with a young girl come in, which set off a new chorus of small dogs barking and yapping for attention.

"Sorry," the woman said. "Are we interrupting something?"

"No, you're fine," Angela said. "We were just chatting about one of the dogs."

"Good. We just came in from looking at all the big dogs. Told my daughter when she was ten, she could get one. None of the bigger ones were doing it for her, so thought we'd see what you had in here."

"That's fine," Kim said. "Feel free to check out our little guys. Did anyone tell you how to read the cards? The ones in those little sleeves on each cage?"

"The girl at the front desk did. Like the different colors

for the different temperaments and personalities of the dogs?" said the mother.

"Yes. But before you put your fingers inside any of the cages, like to pet one or get their attention, you should read the cards first. Mainly to look at the section on Aggression. We don't put out any big dogs with aggression issues on the adoption floor. But since lots of folks don't mind it as much with the little dogs, we make some exceptions. We note on the cards if there are any concerns."

"So, if there's nothing written down, they're okay?"

"Yes," Kim said.

"Hear that, Kaley? I'll check the cards, but maybe you should just keep your hands off the cages altogether."

"Okay, Mom."

Rhonda stepped back from Bailey's cage, whispered to Kim, "Should I hold off on our little experiment till they leave?"

"I think so."

The three women backed further away from the cages to give the mom and her daughter some space.

"So many little dogs," the mother said. "Definitely don't want anything that growls or bites. Don't care how small or cute it is."

"Me, neither," said the daughter.

"Any of these puppies?" asked the mom.

"The ones along the top row are," Angela said. "Of course, none of them are aggressive. Some of them do nip if you put your fingers in the cage."

"Well, that doesn't matter. We aren't in the market for a

puppy. We need something already housebroken. I'll be checking that part of the card real closely."

"I still don't know why we can't have a puppy," the daughter said.

"You do know why. You just don't want to accept it. We're not going over that again. Got plenty of little dogs to look at. Like this one here." She pointed to a dog in the middle row. "Got some beagle in him. You're a cute little fellow." The dog did a play bow and was licking her fingers.

"That one's a female," Angela said.

"She's cute," said the daughter, "but she's not the one."

The mother pulled out the card. "What's wrong with her? No aggression, house broke, loves people."

"Nothing wrong with her. Just not the kind of dog I'm looking for. You said I could pick it out."

"I did. I'm just saying."

The little girl walked along the cages checking each one. Whenever she showed the least bit of interest, the mom quickly pulled out the card. Then the girl would say, *It's not that one*, before she read the first lines.

"Is there something specific you're looking for?" Angela asked. "I know most of the dogs in here pretty well."

"We were watching a dog show on TV a few weeks back, just to help us get an idea of what kind of dog she'd like. Course, we couldn't afford any of them purebred types. But you know, just to get an idea of the look that she liked the best."

"I liked the herding ones the best," the girl said. "After that, the terriers were my favorite."

"Lots of people like those kinds of dogs," Kim said. "When we do get them, they don't last very long."

"Are there any other kind of dog you like besides those?" Angela said.

"Nope, not really," the girl replied.

The mother started walking by the dogs in the bigger pens, but Kim could clearly see none of them met the little girl's criteria.

All except one.

Just then, the mother got to Bailey's pen. And of course, Bailey showed zero interest. "This one's kind of cute," she said. "Little shy, but she kinda looks like a herding dog. A small one." She pulled Bailey's card out of its sleeve.

As she did, the little girl hurried over. "She's got the right look," the girl said. "What's her name?"

"Says Bailey on the card," the mother replied.

The girl started calling out to Bailey in the nicest, kindest voice she had. But Bailey just kept looking away. "Something wrong with her? She sick or something?"

"No," Kim said, "she's just —"

"Don't matter what she is," the mother interrupted. "She is definitely not the one." She put the card back in its sleeve.

"Why not?"

"For starters," the mom said, "she's old. She's eleven. We're not bringing home a dog that might die in a year or two."

"Well," Kim said, "Bailey is eleven, but she's relatively healthy for her age, and dogs that size —"

"I'm sorry, but I'm not bringing home a dog that's older

than my daughter. Besides, says on her card she's not good with kids. Another dealbreaker."

"Well, you're right about Bailey not being great with kids. I wouldn't think she'd be a good fit any—"

"She's not. And it's kinda too bad. Can't see her that good all curled up like that, but she's kinda cute and kinda what my daughter is wanting. But I think we just need to keep looking. There's a couple of other privately-owned shelters we're gonna check out next."

"Sounds like an excellent idea," Kim said, hoping she was effectively suppressing the negative feelings that had started to form inside.

The woman headed for the front door. Her daughter was still standing in front of Bailey's cage. Bailey was ignoring her, of course.

"C'mon, Kaley. I gotta be at work in a couple of hours."

Kim and Angela smiled at her as she walked by then followed her mother out into the hallway.

Once they were gone, to everyone's surprise, Bailey lifted her head, looked around as if to verify they were gone, then returned to her previous position.

"I'd love to know what she's thinking," Rhonda said, smiling.

"Probably the same thing we all are," Angela said.

15

AFTER THE MOTHER AND DAUGHTER HAD GONE, RHONDA walked back to Bailey's pen. She looked at Kim and Angela. "I see what you mean about how hard it's going to be for Bailey to be adopted, especially in this condition."

"More like impossible," Angela said. "Even if she was jumping up and down like the other dogs, when people read that info card and see her age, most of them will be turned off."

"If that doesn't get them," Rhonda said, "not being good with kids or other dogs will do it."

"Well," Kim said, "those things are big deals. But there are still some people — like a retiree living alone — who might adopt her. But not if she stays all shut down like this. That's still job one." She looked at Rhonda. "You still open to trying our experiment?"

Rhonda looked down at Bailey. "You sure she was just grinning at me?"

"Pretty sure. Mostly sure."

"How sure?" Rhonda said.

"How's 99.9%?"

"That's pretty good." Rhonda unlatched the gate. "I'll take those odds." The pillow was still in the corner where she'd left it. Bailey didn't acknowledge Rhonda coming inside the cage. "Hey girl, it's just me again. Just coming for a little visit. Not gonna bother you." Rhonda slid down slowly till she was sitting on the pillow, guiding herself by gripping the chain-link fence. "There we are, girl. See? Everything's okay. I'm just gonna sit here a while."

"So far, so good," Angela said.

Kim stepped up closer to the pen. "Keep talking to her the way you're doing, but lean toward her a few inches. Her body posture is good. I don't see any cause for concern."

"You're a good girl, Bailey," Rhonda said. "Such a good girl. I bet you miss your home, don't you?" At that, Bailey's ears perked right up. Just her ears. She didn't lift her head. "She liked that for some reason."

"She probably recognized the word *home*," Kim said. "See? Her ears just reacted to it again. But probably not a good idea to use that word. We don't want to remind her of things she can't have anymore."

"That's kind of sad," said Rhonda. "So, is a word like that ruined for her forever?"

"No, not for good. Just for now. Hopefully, she'll get past this phase. If we can ever get her re-homed with a new owner, and it's a positive experience, she'll start connecting that word to that new experience."

Rhonda thought of what she could say, hoping not to

accidentally say something else in Bailey's vocabulary that might confuse her. Leaning forward as Kim had suggested, she said, "You're such a pretty girl, Bailey. And you have such sweet eyes, did you know that?"

Bailey's head lifted. She looked at Rhonda and exposed her teeth. Rhonda had to keep from laughing, now that she knew this look was supposed to be a grin.

"Look," Angela said, "she's doing it. That's her grinning, right?" she asked Kim.

Kim nodded. "Yep. That's the Aussie grin. She's not making any sound, right? She's not growling?"

"No," Rhonda said. "She's just smiling away at me, aren't you girl? Yes. What a pretty smile you have." Bailey lifted her head a little more and turned it more toward Rhonda.

"I'm sorry," said Angela. "But that is not a pretty smile."

Kim laughed.

"If you weren't here telling me this is a grin, I'd still think it was a sign of aggression."

"But look at her eyes," Kim said. "Totally soft. She's not tensing up, or pulling back."

"Such a good girl," Rhonda said. Bailey stopped grinning but was still looking at Rhonda. Her face did look very soft and sweet. "It almost seems like I could reach out and pet her."

"You almost could," Kim said. "But let's take it slow. I've got an idea. Angela, do you have those treats her owner gave us, the ones he said were her favorites?"

Angela walked over to her desk. "Got them in my top drawer, in a baggie with her name on them." She opened the drawer. "Here they are."

"Could you hand me one?"

"Here's two," Angela said.

Kim walked forward slowly, holding one of the treats out between two fingers. She slid it through the opening in the fence. "Let's try this, Rhonda. Her owner said she absolutely loved these. We've tried to give them to her before, but she showed no interest. Let's see how she responds if you give it to her."

Rhonda kept her gaze on Bailey, trying to look as pleasant as she could, while she reached back for the treat. She felt it in her fingers and slowly brought it around in front of her. Holding it out so Bailey could see it, she said, "Look at this, Bailey. Remember these?"

Bailey grinned again.

Everyone laughed. Rhonda quickly stifled hers. "You do. You like treats. These treats are your favorites." Rhonda saw her ears perk right up. "Guess she knows that word, too."

"I saw that, too," Kim said. "But that's a word we can keep using. You know why?"

"Because it brings up a good memory," Rhonda said, "and because it's not something she's lost."

"Exactly. Do you see her staring at it? Slowly hold it out to her, see what happens."

Rhonda did. Bailey didn't pull back. She stopped grinning, but her eyes stayed focused on the treat. When the gap closed to a couple of inches, Bailey gently took the treat in her mouth, as Rhonda let go. She immediately began gobbling it up.

"Well, would you look at that?" Angela said.

"Here's the other one." Kim slid it through the fence to Rhonda.

Rhonda did just as she had done with the first one. Sure enough, Bailey ate that one just as quickly. "You're a hungry girl, aren't you? But you took that so nicely. You're such a sweet thing, aren't you Bailey?"

Then Bailey did something no one expected. She wagged her little nub of a tail. Ever so slightly, but it was definitely wagging.

"I can hardly believe it," Kim said. "Rhonda, no one's been able to get any positive progress with her since the moment she was dropped off."

"Do you think I should try to pet her now?"

"No," Kim said. "Don't want to push too hard the first time. Let's try that the next time you come."

"Can I come back tomorrow?" Rhonda said.

"If you'd like," Kim said. "That would be great for Bailey, if you could."

"I definitely will." She looked back at Bailey. "I'm gonna get up now girl. But you're fine. You'll be okay. I'll see you again tomorrow." She quietly got up and eased herself out of the cage.

"Well," Angela said, "that went way better than I expected."

"I agree," Kim said. She looked at Rhonda. "You did great."

"Thanks." Now, Rhonda was grinning. On the inside, too. She didn't know why, but this seemed like a significant achievement.

It was silly, but still, it did.

16

Kim walked back to her office feeling pretty upbeat. They were still a long way off from finding Bailey a new home, but this little progress step with Rhonda was certainly encouraging. Time would tell how much further Bailey would come out of her shell, but until a few moments ago, it seemed she might be a lost cause.

Kim walked in and found Amy typing away on her computer. "What are you working on so furiously?"

Amy sighed. "Just trying to get caught up on my emails. Well, my emails and my Facebook messages, and all the other ways people interact with you these days. Do you remember when we were kids? Didn't it seem so much simpler back then?"

Kim took a seat. "Are we talking about communication, or about life in general?"

"Communication," Amy said. "Social media. Sometimes, I think I was born in the wrong era. Because I really hate all this. I know as a millennial, I'm supposed to be all jazzed about technology and all the exciting things made possible by the digital age. But, I'm just not. In the last few weeks, Chris and I got into watching a bunch of different British dramas set in the 1800s. Some are murder mysteries, some are more romantic sagas. But when I watch them I get totally sucked in."

"You mean like Jane Austen movies?" Kim said.

"I like those, too. But these are different ones. We've been trying out one of those Brit streaming channels. They've made so many series set in that time period. Guess most are based on books, but by authors I've never heard of. But the stories are really fun. Even Chris is liking them, and I can never get him to watch Hallmark movies. The point is...I can really see how simple things were back then compared to now. And in some ways, it seems better somehow. Obviously, some of the technology stuff we have now has made life a lot easier."

"Like toilets that flush," Kim said.

Amy laughed. "Yeah, like that. "And air conditioning. Don't think I could live without A/C. Not in Florida anyhow."

"Lights that turn on with a switch," Kim said.

"Okay, that too. Although I kinda like the way rooms look lit by candlelight. But I'm talking about the way people communicated back then. Or in one sense, the *limits* they had when they communicated with each other." She looked back at her computer screen. "Look at this list of emails I've gotten, just in the last twenty-four hours. When you delete out the dozens that got past my junk mail filters, there's at least fifteen or twenty from people whose dogs I've trained complaining about something, or looking for some free advice. Whether by email, or by text, or using social media, anyone who has a stray thought, an idle curiosity, or some other reason to want to reach me, it's the easiest thing in the world for them to do. In the 1800s, not one of these people would be able to connect with me. It simply wasn't possible."

"That's true," Kim said. "Not a single one."

"And would that be so awful?" Amy said. "I've already answered five of these. None of them were significant things. If any of these people had to walk across town to tell me their thought or ask me a question, they'd instantly realize it wasn't worth the energy or the time. And they'd drop it. Life would go on. No harm done. But all they have to do is take two minutes to type out their message and click a button, and voilà...it becomes something I have to respond to."

"You've given this quite a lot of thought," Kim said.

"Guess I have."

"Have you also thought about this...without all these people bothering you, on all these different social platforms, you wouldn't have a job? I don't imagine back in the 1800s there were too many women earning a living as dog trainers."

Amy smiled. "No, I suppose not."

"Wouldn't imagine there were too many dog owners willing to walk all the way across town — if they even had any dog trainers — to set up an appointment for a lesson."

"That's probably true, too. I probably wouldn't be able to be a dog trainer," Amy said.

"No, and you'd probably spend your entire morning hand washing your dirty clothes down by the stream, or whatever other primitive means they had to use back then. Your entire day would be spent exhausting yourself cleaning and cooking and doing all the other chores they had to do by hand back then. And when the day was finally over, you and Chris wouldn't get to sit down cuddling on a comfortable couch watching British period dramas together on TV. A huge flat screen, high-def TV."

Amy laughed. "Okay, that would be pretty awful. Maybe we don't have to lose *all* the technology. Just go back a few decades before we had social media. Far enough to cut back on all this pointless communication I have to fiddle with every day."

"A much more sensible fantasy," Kim said.

"Well, thanks for listening to my rant. Better get back to reality." She looked at her screen. "Let's see. Here's the next one. *My dog keeps rubbing his butt on my carpet. How do I make him stop?*"

Kim laughed. "Think of the difference you could make in that woman's life."

Amy started typing out her response. Kim checked her own email inbox but soon found herself drifting into her own kind of fantasy. In some ways, she envied Amy being able to spend her evenings cuddling on the couch with Chris watching old British movies on TV. That's what young married couples did. And other things after that, if they wanted. And she wished that Ned had a similar fantasy, and that this fantasy might inspire him to want to get married.

Not fifteen years from now. Or five years from now. But soon. Very soon.

Just then her phone rang.

It was Ned. She sighed. It's not that she wasn't glad he called. Just the opposite...she wanted to be with him all the time.

She picked up her phone. "Hey, Ned. How's it going?"

"Had a pretty good day," he said. "But it would be an even better day if it could end with me taking you out to a fancy restaurant for dinner. Not the kind we usually go to. But a really nice one, where it costs way too much for even the cheap stuff on the menu. The kind you have to get a little dressed up for. Are you up for that?"

She smiled. "I totally am. Did you come into some money?"

"Don't tell anyone. I busted a drug dealer. He had this big suitcase in the back seat."

"Ned..."

"Don't you worry about the money. You're worth it. I'll pick you up at seven."

17

KIM STOOD OUTSIDE ON THE FRONT STEPS ENJOYING THE COOL evening breeze. She glanced at her watch, which confirmed Ned should be here any minute. That's one thing she'd learned about him early on...Ned liked to be places on time. And if something did keep him from being with her when he was supposed to — usually his job — he always called. He told her once he did that to keep her from worrying something might have happened. The implication seemed to be, with a job like his that was a possibility.

She tried not to think about that too much. Ned generally shared with her everything he could about what had gone on during his shifts when they got together. Living in a town like Summerville, the majority of his stories were fairly mild. Ned said there was little chance they'd ever film a reality show like Cops in Summerville. Which, of course, was perfectly fine with Kim.

She was very curious to find out what, if anything, had prompted Ned to want to go out for dinner tonight. Eating out wasn't that unusual. They did it about once a week, sometimes more. It was the getting-dressed-up-and-eating-at-someplace-expensive part that piqued her interest. Ned wasn't a cheapskate. He figured if they ate at more moderately-priced places they'd be able to do it more often.

Kim was fine with that. They'd been to a lot of places so far, some several times, and she'd always enjoyed it. And he was old-fashioned about never letting her pay. She was fine with that, too.

She looked up in time to see his car coming around the corner and started walking toward the street. As he slowed to pull in next to the curb, he saw her through the windshield. A startled look appeared on his face, then a very big smile. She could see he was wearing that nice blue dress shirt he sometimes wore to church. He put the car in park but left it running as he opened the door.

"My goodness, look at you," he said. "Have I ever seen you in that dress before?"

"I don't think you have. I've never worn it when we've been out."

"Well, you'll have to wear that more often."

"You'll have to take me out to fancy places more often, I guess." She smiled.

"Guess I will then." He walked around the front of the car while she waited by the passenger side door. He hugged her and gave her a nice kiss, lingering a little longer than normal. "You hungry?" He opened her door, and she got in.

"Starving. Not to mention curious. My taste buds don't know what to expect, since you haven't said where we're going."

He closed her door and headed back around the front, got in beside her. "When I called, I couldn't say until I'd confirmed a few details. Now I can tell you. Every been to Villa de Palma?"

"Villa de Palma?" she said. "No, but I know my parents have...on very special occasions. They've been going there off and on for years. My mom raves about it. It's a buffet, right?"

He put the car in gear and started driving. "Yeah, but not like any buffet you've ever been to. My parents took me when I graduated from the police academy. I'm telling you... that might've been the best night of eating I've ever had. They rotate between three or four different themes during the week. But I've heard none of them are duds. Tonight, it's Mediterranean cuisine night. That's what it was when I went there and what I was hoping for, because it's so good."

"I'm not sure what Mediterranean food is."

"Me, either," Ned said. "But if it's what I had that night, I know you're gonna love it. I mean, there's so many different things to pick from. And every one of them is gourmet quality. Like you see on those cooking shows."

"Sounds exciting. What was your favorite thing?"

"Probably the coconut mango shrimp. They were amazing, and they had this dipping sauce that went perfectly with it. But I also liked their salmon. I've had salmon before, but it was nothing like this. And it also had this amazing sauce on top. If you're in the mood for beef, they have prime rib every night. A guy right there slices it however you like. Even the salad bar was amazing. I would go to this place just for that."

Kim loved seafood and prime rib and a good salad bar. This was gonna be a fun night of eating. "My only problem with buffets is I can never seem to eat more than one plate. So, the all-you-can-eat part is kinda wasted on me."

"Well," Ned said, "I get that. I can't eat near as much at a buffet like I used to. So, I don't make it about how much I can eat but getting a nice variety. You know, sampling stuff. Especially on your first trip. Just take a little bit of everything that appeals to you. Then you can go back and get more of the ones you really like. Another trick is, a place like this is for dining. You know, taking things nice and slow. The waiters never rush you. I guess because they get such great tips at every table. So, we can take our time. If we don't have room for dessert, we'll just have coffee and chat a while till we make some room."

Kim liked the sound of that. That was another reason why she loved spending time with Ned. He really liked to talk. And he listened just as much. "So, what were the details you had to confirm?"

"What?"

"You know, you said you couldn't tell me before where we were going until you confirmed some details?"

"Oh, uh...nothing much. Like, wanting to make sure it was Mediterranean night. And that we could get in at seven without waiting too long."

Kim knew Ned hated waiting in long lines at restaurants. She looked over at him, caught him glancing at her. He smiled then quickly faced the road again. But there was a look in his eyes she couldn't quite figure out.

Like he had something else to say but had changed his mind.

18

WHEN THEY ARRIVED AT VILLA DE PALMA, IT WAS AS ELEGANT close-up as she imagined driving by on the road. The decor seemed drawn from what she remembered on one of several visits to historic St. Augustine, the oldest city in the US. To her surprise, Ned pulled into the section for valet parking. "You're really going to splurge."

"You only live once, right? Can't come to a place like this and park your own car. People would talk."

She laughed. "Think they'll be talking anyway, Ned, starting with the valet drivers when they park your car next to all the BMWs and Audis in the valet lot."

"I know," he said. "I'm not doing this for anyone but you."

That was sweet. "Well, I appreciate it. I haven't had valet service at a restaurant since..." She just remembered when.

"Since you were dating that billionaire?" Ned said, as he got out of the car.

The valet opened the door for her and she got out. They had talked about her relationship with Taylor Saunders before, but she didn't like bringing it up just the same. "Yes, now that you mention it."

He handed the valet his keys, came around the car, and took her hand. "Did you guys eat at a lot at places like this?"

"We didn't date for that many months, but yes, when we did eat out it was always at places like this, or..."

"Better," Ned said.

"Well, I don't know about better, but definitely more expensive. But I guess the most expensive meals we ate were the ones prepared by his chef when we flew on his private plane." They reached the front door, opened for them by a hostess.

"I can't even fathom living like that," Ned said.

They walked into the lobby, which was more like a glass atrium. Kim loved all the indoor palms and tropical plants. "I couldn't either. It was really one of the main reasons why we broke up. He was a decent guy, but I just couldn't fit in with that kind of lifestyle. What was very normal and every day for him just kept freaking me out, like all the time. And I knew this pretty early on, so we parted as friends before things got serious."

"So, this isn't, like, a letdown for you?" Ned said.

"Ned, this is amazing. I already like it better than any of the places where Taylor and I had dinner. Because I'm here with you."

He got the biggest smile. "That deserves a kiss." So, he did.

"A couple in love," a young woman's voice said. "What

we love to see here at Villa de Palma. Do you have a reservation?"

"We do. At 7:20, for Ned Barrington."

The hostess looked at her screen. "Yes, got it right here. And I see your table is all ready for you. Our hostess, Anita, will take you there. Have a lovely dinner."

An attractive Hispanic girl stepped up to greet them. Kim saw her name tag. Clearly, Anita. Ned followed behind her as she walked into the restaurant, Kim still holding his hand.

"That section over there on the far wall is the buffet area," Ned said, as they walked. "It starts with the salad bar and breads on the right, all homemade. The entrées are in the middle. And there's the guy who grills your beef to order. And that whole roundish area on the left end are the desserts."

"Can't wait to try it," she said.

Anita brought them to their table, a very comfortable booth. Kim looked around. The dining area was about half full. She'd heard it was packed on weekends.

"The hardest part for me is not getting stuffed at that first section," Ned said. "You'll have to try at least one of the breads."

"I will." Kim loved how excited he was getting.

A handsome Latino man dressed like all the other waiters came up. He instantly started pouring their waters from a glass pitcher. "Good evening everyone. My name is Marco. I'll be your waiter this evening. Have either of you ever been with us before?"

"I haven't," Kim said. "My parents have, many times."

"I've been a few times," Ned said. "Always on Mediterranean night, on purpose."

"I understand," said Marco. "It's my personal favorite, as well. Would either of you care for some wine, or some other drink?"

"Just unsweet tea," Ned said. "With lemon."

"Same for me."

"Very well. As you can see, there are sugar and other sweeteners in the center of the table. I'm sure you're both hungry, so make your way to the buffet. The plates are up there by the food. I'll be right back with your tea."

For the next ninety minutes, Kim and Ned made several trips back and forth to the buffet. Kim did as Ned had suggested, taking small samples of everything that appealed to her. The problem was, everything she took was amazing, as good as everything else on the plate. So, she decided to go back for things she knew she would never get except in a place like this.

She passed on the prime rib, knowing it would fill her up all by itself. Even though Ned got more food than she did at the buffet, he couldn't refuse the prime rib, but happily shared several bites with her. It tasted like filet mignon, it was so tender.

The conversation, as always with Ned, flowed easily. Lots of the kind of catching up they usually did with each other, filling in all the details of the various stories that took place at work. She filled him in on the whole Bailey saga, drawing comparisons to his experience rescuing Parker some months ago. Although, in some ways, Parker had come out of his dilemma more quickly than Bailey. She could only hope Bailey would make the kind of full recovery Parker had.

Ned had shared with her about a recent visit with his mom. No special reason, he'd said, just wanting to stay in touch. She liked that about Ned, too. Very committed to his folks. That led into him telling her more about his siblings, whom she'd only met a handful of times. They both agreed to make a better effort to visit his family more often going forward. For some reason, they probably visited her family three to one over his.

Marco came up to their table. He'd done an amazing job of keeping the table cleared, while giving them all kinds of space to talk. "Can I get those plates for you? I noticed neither of you have been eating the last ten minutes or so."

"Just saving up room for dessert, Marco," Ned said. "But yes, we're done with these. I think I'm ready for dessert now." He looked at Kim.

"I'm willing to give it a try," she said. "I did see a few things I'd like to at least taste. Like that flan, for one."

"Our flan is wonderful," Marco said. "You do have to try it, if nothing else."

"Okay," she said, "you sold me." She got up, and so did Ned.

"I'll be there in a minute," he said. "Just want to make a quick trip to the restroom."

Kim took one of the dessert plates, got a serving of that flan but then couldn't resist the tiramisu, or a small slice of the chocolate mousse. And they had these mini cannolis, with several different fillings. She picked one of each of those.

Pangs of guilt tormented her as she walked back to the table. She'd never be able to eat all this. It was enough dessert to last a week. She looked up and saw Ned at the table talking to Marco. She hadn't seen him at the dessert buffet. He looked, saw her, nodded to Marco and she heard Marco thanking him profusely as she got closer.

Ned looked at her plate and smiled. "I knew that would happen. Isn't that what I said, Marco?"

"It is, sir. I will leave you both to enjoy your dessert." He walked away.

"Is that what you were talking about? How much food is on my plate?"

"Kinda. I was about to join you then thought about this." He pointed at her plate. "I asked the waiter if it'd be okay if you could bring home whatever was left. Buffets usually don't allow that. He told me this restaurant knows its clientele isn't here to steal food, so they'd have no problem with that."

"What was he thanking you for as I walked up?"

"Oh, I just told him what an amazing job he did tonight, and that my gratitude would be reflected in my tip." He looked down at her plate again. "I better go get some of that good stuff. I'll be right back."

By the time he returned, Kim had eaten most of the flan. It was so good. As he sat, she was almost embarrassed by his plate. About half the amount she'd picked. "Now you're making me feel bad."

"No reason you should. I ate at least a whole plate more food from the main buffet than you did."

They continued to eat dessert and sip their coffee. But it didn't take long before Ned asked, "You there yet?"

"I should've been there several bites ago, but yes. I'm there."

Ned signaled Marco who came right over. He set down the bill. "Let me take your dessert plates. I'll put what's left in separate boxes," he said. "If that's okay."

"That'll be great, Marco. And here, might as well take this, too." Ned put his credit card in the bill folder and handed it back.

"Very good. I'll be back in a few moments."

"I really want to thank you, Ned. For doing this," Kim said. "It's not even a special occasion, but you did it anyway."

He smiled. "It's always a special occasion for me, getting to go out with you. I almost lost you a while back, remember?"

She did, back when she wasn't sure she could handle him being a policeman. "I was just confused about things for a little while."

"Still," Ned said. He reached for her hand across the table, and she held his. "Made me realize when you came back, how much I...well, here comes the waiter. I'll finish what I was going to say in a sec."

Marco set their individual containers down in front of them. Handed Ned the bill folder with the receipt that now included his credit card info. He stood back a few steps. Ned quickly filled it out and signed it, handed it back and stood.

Kim stood and backed away from her chair.

As she took hold of her dessert box, Marco said, "You

know what? Maybe you should double-check what's inside, to make sure I didn't mix them up in the kitchen."

"Okay." She picked hers up and opened the lid. She was stunned by what she saw inside. "Oh, my gosh." Tears began to fill her eyes. She tried blinking them away. In the center of the container was a black velvety box, the lid already opened. Inside was a glistening diamond ring.

Ned took Kim's hand and, dropping to one knee, said, "Kim Harper, when you came back to me, it made me realize how miserable I was and how empty my life would be without you. I've loved you from day one. And if you'll have me, I'll love you with everything I've got for the rest of our lives. Will you marry me?"

"YES!" she almost yelled, "of course, I'll marry you." She set the dessert box down on the table and leaned forward to kiss him. As she did, Ned began to stand and now took her in his arms and kissed her even harder. Several couples nearby began to clap.

He looked into her eyes. "I love you, Kim."

"I love you, too."

They kissed again.

"Here," he said. "Let's get this thing on your finger." He reached down and pulled the ring out of the velvet box. She held out her hand, and he slipped it on. "It belonged to my grandmother. You would have loved her if she was still here."

"It's perfect, Ned. I totally love it." She held it out and looked at it again, then gave him another hug.

Ned looked over at Marco. "Thank you so much, my friend."

He handed Ned's phone back. "You are most welcome. I got a lot of great pictures. Congratulations to the both of you. So glad I could play a small part in your special moment."

They walked out to the front door holding hands. Every few moments, Kim looked at her other hand.

The one with the ring on it.

19

THE FOLLOWING MORNING, KIM COULDN'T WAIT TO GET INTO her office and show Amy her ring. In some ways, it still hadn't sunk in...that she was engaged now. It was really happening. She had no misgivings or doubts about saying yes. It was just...she had been living as a single woman for quite a few years now and had grown used to the idea and all the routines that go along with being on your own.

But she was more than ready for the exchange.

Ned had already texted her twice that morning. The first one was short and sweet: *Thanks...for saying yes.* She'd almost texted back: *You're welcome,* but said instead: *Thanks...for asking.* The second one came just before she got into the car. It was a little longer: *I can't wait until we're together all the time. Can we not make this a long engagement?* She texted back: *Me, too. Just need enough time to plan the wedding. Let's chat about that soon.*

That second text made her realize how unprepared she

was. Not to be married, just the wedding itself. She'd have to find out what Ned wanted. She was pretty sure he'd want a church wedding, but they hadn't discussed anything specific. She didn't need or want a big wedding. Maybe if she had gotten married years ago when she still had all her connections from school. But now, other than a handful of people here at the shelter and her direct family, Kim's guest list was small.

Then there was the question of money. Who would be footing the bill? Traditionally, the bride's parents picked up most of the cost. She had no idea if her father even had the money set aside for something like this. She'd have to ask her mom.

That's right, her mom. She didn't get to call her folks last night, since she and Ned had eaten kind of late then took their time at the restaurant. Her mom would be thrilled at this news. In the months they had dated, she had really grown to love Ned. Love might be too strong a word to use with her dad. But she could tell he at least liked Ned a great deal.

She opened her office door and was instantly greeted by Finley. Amy was on the phone but looked up and smiled. Kim bent down to return Finley's affection properly. "How's my boy this morning? Thank you for coming to say hi." She stood but continued to pat his head. She loved how he leaned his head against her leg. "I'm so glad you're here today. Feels like I haven't seen you in a week."

He followed her over as she sat at her desk and turned on her computer. He wasn't quite ready for their encounter to end. But then again, Finley was a lover. He could never get enough attention and never tired giving affection in return.

Amy hung up the phone. "Okay Finley, that's enough, buddy. Give Kim a chance to settle in."

Finley got the basic gist and returned to Amy's desk and laid down on the dog bed beside it.

"So..." Amy said, "how did your big date go last night? Villa De Palma, I'm jealous. I asked Chris why he's never taken me there. You know what he said?"

"No."

"Because I'm a groundskeeper at a golf course, not a golf pro. Oh well," she said, "maybe someday our ship will come in. Was it everything you imagined?"

"Way more," Kim said. Should she just tell her? She decided to just talk about it like a regular date, see how long it took Amy to notice the ring. "The place was so nice. Everything about it is first class. Reminded me of the kind of places Taylor used to take me to."

"That's right," Amy said. "The mega billionaire you let get away. So, how was the food? What did you order?"

"The food was incredible, but I didn't order anything. It's a buffet."

"That's right. I forgot. Every buffet I've ever eaten at wasn't, well, let's just say...there was plenty of food."

"There was certainly plenty of food," Kim said. "But imagine going to an upscale, gourmet restaurant with a full menu but everything on the menu was laid out in a buffet. That's what this was like. Everything — from the bread to the dessert — was delicious. Like the best food on earth."

She went on to explain all the various things she tried, the ones she enjoyed the most. All the while using her hands while she spoke, more than she'd usually do. But somehow, Amy didn't see the ring.

"Well, I'm just going to have to find a way to get there with Chris," Amy said. "So, did Ned ever explain why he chose last night to take you to such an expensive —"

That's when it happened. Amy saw the ring.

"Oh, my gosh. Is that what I think it is?"

Kim was bursting inside. She held her hand out, so Amy could see it plainly. "Yes, it is! And I didn't have to wait fifteen years."

Amy got teary-eyed, and quickly jumped from her chair to hug Kim. "I can't believe it. No, I can believe it. I just didn't think it would happen so soon."

Finley jumped up and instantly started trying to comfort the women, wrongly interpreting the mood.

"Let me see it," Amy said, pulling out of the hug. She turned to Finley. "We're okay, boy. See? Happy face. Everything's okay."

Kim held her hand out. "It was his grandmother's ring. I love all the little artistic engravings on either side. You never see that on engagement rings anymore. And I especially love where it came from."

"Oh, Kim. I'm so happy for you, and for Ned. He's getting to marry the best person I know. You know what this means? Pretty soon we can start going places as old married couples. It'll be such fun." She sat back in her chair. "Okay, now tell me how he proposed. Tell me everything, from beginning to end."

20

AFTER TELLING AMY THE WHOLE STORY AND GETTING organized for the day, Kim decided to check in on Bailey, see how she was doing. Opening the door to the Small Dog area, she walked in and found Angela changing water bowls in the cages. Of course, the dogs were going nuts. And of course, everyone but Bailey. "Any responses from her today?"

Angela looked over. "You mean Bailey? About the same. Although I haven't tried to engage her yet in any direct way. Been kind of busy with my morning routine."

"That's okay, I was just curious. Is Rhonda still coming in this morning?"

"As far as I know."

Kim noticed the floor pillow Rhonda had used in Bailey's cage was back on the shelf. She decided to leave it there. Bailey wasn't near ready for Kim to invade her space that closely. She walked over and stood in front of Bailey, a few feet back from the door. There she was, in her typical shutdown position. Kim looked at her bowl. "Are you feeding her less than you used to?"

"No," Angela said, "same as I've been feeding her all along."

"Well, Bailey." Kim came closer and squatted down. "Guess you're getting your appetite back. A little bit anyway." She turned and looked at Angela over her shoulder. "Her bowl's half-empty."

"Really? That's some progress."

"Definitely a good sign," Kim said. "After how it's been, I'll take any progress." She refocused on Bailey. "That's such a good girl. Glad to see you're starting to eat." Still no reaction. "Hey, Angela? How does Bailey react when you change her water?"

"Pretty much ignores me. Stays in that curled up position in the corner. Of course, I stopped trying to interact with her a while ago."

"I think I'll change her water myself, see how she responds." She walked over to Angela's cart and grabbed one of the water jugs. Stepping very slowly, she made her way back to Bailey's cage and quietly opened the front door. "It's just me, girl. Everything's okay. Just changing your water. You know that word? Water?" Bailey's ears perked up briefly. "Figured you did. Every dog knows about water. Just giving you some fresh water."

Her water bowl was nearly empty. "I guess you were thirsty, after eating that food. Let's give you some more." Kim put down the water bowl. Bailey actually watched her, which meant she had to turn her head in Kim's direction.

"What a good girl," she said in her most soothing tone. "You remember me, don't you girl? I was there the first day. Remember how you let me pet you and hold you?" Kim knew it was only because Bailey had been terrified by the encounter. "What a good girl you are."

Then Bailey did it. She gave Kim an Aussie grin.

"Well look at that?" Kim said. "Such a pretty smile." Kim tried to interpret what was behind it. Was she nervous? Feeling intimidated? Happy to see Kim? As best she could tell, Bailey wasn't tensing up. Kim wanted so bad to pet her but decided not to chance it.

Just then the door opened. It was Rhonda. To Kim's surprise, Bailey lifted her head and turned to face Rhonda. Her tail wagged. This was a very good sign. "Rhonda, good morning. Why don't you put your things down and come on over here. Somebody's almost excited to see you."

"Really?" Rhonda said and hurried over.

BAILEY THOUGHT she heard that lady's voice. The nice one who came into her space yesterday. The woman with her now also seemed nice, but Bailey remembered...she was there that day when she'd been taken away from Harold. But the other lady...yes, there she was, coming this way.

The woman in her cage got up slowly. "Okay, Bailey. I'm going to go out now. Rhonda's here. I can tell you remember her."

"Look at that," Angela said. "She's looking right at Rhonda. And no funny grin."

Kim exited the pen and closed it over without latching

it. "She's all yours. Wish I could stay longer, but I'm needed elsewhere."

Bailey looked up. The first woman was leaving the room. She hoped the other one, the one from yesterday, would take her place.

A few moments later. Yes, she was. She was coming inside.

She wasn't anything compared to Harold, but in some ways her voice reminded Bailey of Alice, the woman who'd lived with Harold for so many years. This woman didn't look or smell anything like Alice, but she definitely made Bailey think of her. And that was a good thing.

"Good morning, Bailey," Rhonda said. "I'm so glad I came back. Look at you looking at me. Such a good girl." Rhonda set the pillow down the exact spot it had occupied yesterday and slowly sat down.

Bailey felt something inside she hadn't felt for so long. Something almost like happiness. Her tail began to wag even harder, she couldn't help it. She wondered if this woman would touch her, maybe pat her on the head. She missed being touched so much. She thought maybe she was ready. But not for just anyone.

Just this lady.

The one in here with her now.

Bailey had to keep listening, see if she could figure out her name.

21

RHONDA WAS ALMOST BESIDE HERSELF WITH EXCITEMENT. A dog reacting positively to your presence should probably not matter this much, but it did. "I wonder if she'd let me pet her. It almost seems like I could."

"You probably could," Angela said. "Didn't Kim say yesterday you could try the next time you came in?"

"She did say that."

"But wait a sec," said Angela. "Just for curiosity's sake, before you try it, let's see how she responds to me when I come over. I won't come in the cage, just stand nearby."

"Okay."

Rhonda watched Angela slowly come this way. She could instantly sense Bailey begin to shut down. Before Angela reached Bailey's gate, she completely turned away and resumed her old, familiar position.

"Well, guess we don't have to wonder anymore," Angela said. "Clearly, she wants nothing to do with me."

Rhonda looked down at Bailey. "I wonder why she's acting this way? It's not like you've ever done anything mean to her."

"I'm okay with it. I don't take it personally. I kind of expected her to react this way. Although I was hoping the way she responded to you might have broken some kind of spell, and she'd be like that to everyone."

"Looks like we're not there yet," Rhonda said. She was about to suggest maybe Angela should back away when Angela did on her own. As soon as she did, Bailey noticed and looked up, as if to make sure she was really gone.

"You're okay, Bailey," Angela said. "I won't bother you none."

"Sorry," Rhonda said.

"Don't be. Ride the wave as far as it will go. See if you can get her responding again, then pick the moment and pet her. See what happens."

"Okay, I will." She refocused her gaze on Bailey. "It's okay, girl. You don't have to do anything you're not ready for. We can just sit in here for a while, if you want." Bailey's tail started wagging again. She looked back up at Rhonda and grinned.

Rhonda laughed. She couldn't help it. It was such a silly sight. "We're going to have to work on that smile of yours, aren't we? Can't have you scaring people off when they come to visit."

"If we get to the place where Bailey's starting to pay attention to anyone else but you," Angela said, "I'll make sure to tell them about that Aussie grin thing, now that I know what it is. Because that dog doesn't need any additional deal breakers. She's got plenty, as it is."

Rhonda hated hearing Angela say this, though she knew it was true. She could clearly see Bailey really was such a sweet animal. She was just lonely, confused, and afraid. "Say Angela, could you do me a favor? Should have thought of this before I came in here, but could you grab me a handful of those treats we used yesterday?"

"Sure thing." A few moments later, Angela slipped them to Rhonda through the openings in the fence.

Bailey's eyes instantly reacted to the treats. "You want one of these, Bailey? Here you go." This time Rhonda held it in the palm of her hand as she extended it toward Bailey. Bailey's head pulled back a little, but only a little. She obviously wanted it, so Rhonda left her hand extended just a few inches from her mouth. "It's okay, girl. You can have it. The whole thing. Take it."

A few seconds later, Bailey stuck her neck out and reached for the treat, nibbling it with her front teeth.

"That's it. You can have it."

She gobbled it up.

"Good girl. Want another?" She held one up in front of Bailey's face. "Who's a good girl?" Her tail started to wag. "That's right, it's for you. Here." Again, she put it in the palm of her hand only this time Bailey took it without any hesitation.

Rhonda chose that moment to pat the side of Bailey's head, gently. To her delight, Bailey leaned her head into Rhonda's hand...just the way Rhonda's Amos used to do. She knew it meant he liked it, which meant Bailey was liking this, too. So, Rhonda went a little further and started scratching behind her right ear. Now Bailey turned her head a little sideways, as if to make sure Rhonda was hitting the right spot. "You like that, girl? Guess it's been a while since you had anyone do this, hasn't it?"

Now Rhonda moved her hand slowly underneath her chin. Bailey rested it in her hand, so Rhonda began scratching it also.

"Can't believe what I'm seeing," Angela said, while still keeping her distance. "Guess she's making up for lost time."

"I know," Rhonda said. "It's like all of a sudden we're good friends. Think I could try taking her for a walk?"

"I can't see why not. We should know very quickly if it's a good or a bad idea by the way she reacts to the leash. Here, I'll bring it to you." Angela walked over to a row of hooks on a wall by the front door and picked a nice red one.

Rhonda looked at Bailey. "Want to go for a walk, Bailey? Would you like that? Go for a walk?"

Bailey lifted her head and her ears perked up. She noticed Angela heading this way and her demeanor changed. She didn't shut all the way down but definitely got a little more nervous.

"How about I just hand you the handle through the opening here," Angela said, "and you pull it through the rest of the way. I'm afraid I'll lose her completely if I open the gate."

"Sure," said Rhonda, "let's try that. You're okay, Bailey. See, just a leash. Want to go for a walk? A walk?" She pulled the leash all the way through as she talked. Bailey calmed back down when Angela moved back to her desk. She focused on the leash. Rhonda held the clip up and snapped it a couple of times. Bailey stood right up. So quickly, it surprised Rhonda.

"Guess you're going for a walk," Angela said.

"I guess we are." Rhonda stood up and held the clip toward Bailey. She didn't back away. Instead, she came forward and lifted her head, almost inviting Rhonda to clip it on. "Good girl, Bailey. Let's go for a walk. What do you say, girl? Just you and me."

She opened Bailey's gate and stepped out into the room. Bailey followed right behind her, pretty as you please.

Angela just shook her head. "Kim is not gonna believe this."

22

BAILEY WAS ACTUALLY ENJOYING THIS.

This nice woman had come back again, and it was obvious that she'd come back to see Bailey. Bailey liked her face, her smile, her voice, and especially how calm she was. So, she decided...maybe it would be okay to be with her now. She mostly wanted to see Harold again and be back in her home, the only home she had ever known. She didn't know why that couldn't happen, why Harold and Bill had left her here, or why they had never come back.

It wasn't just missing Harold that was so upsetting. It was also the total confusion brought on by losing all her familiar routines. Back at the old place, everything made sense.

Here, nothing did.

But now this nice woman was taking her out of this terrible place. They were going for a walk. Bailey had heard that word as soon as it was said and recognized it immediately. Even though it had been so long since Harold had brought her on one. She used to love going on walks with him. They used to do them almost every day. Then something happened, and they stopped. She'd still be able to go outside in the backyard through the doggy door. But that wasn't even close to the joy she felt when he'd take her for a walk.

Bailey looked around and sniffed the air, trying to figure out where they were. It wasn't far from that awful place, but at least they were moving away from it. She still could see far too many dogs being walked nearby, which made her nervous. At least they were all on leashes, so it wasn't likely that any of them would attack.

"You're doing great, Bailey," the woman said. "Not pulling at all. Somebody must've trained you well."

Bailey didn't know what she just said but liked the way it sounded and the look on her face. Just then, Bailey got the urge. She tried to ignore it, but it was too strong. She stepped off the sidewalk onto the grass and squatted.

"What's the matter? Oh, excuse me. I didn't see you had to go. At least it's just number one. I guess we'll walk to that fenced-in area then turn around and head back. How's that sound?"

They continued walking a few more minutes but, so far, Bailey didn't see any houses nearby. She wondered where this woman lived. They reached a fence, walked around it, then started walking back the way they came.

"Great job Bailey. You're doing wonderful."

Bailey didn't understand. The woman seemed just as happy as before, but for some reason they were heading back toward the big building. To the awful place. A few minutes more, and Bailey was certain. That's where they were headed.

But why? She didn't understand. She started to slow down until now the nice woman was well in front of her. But still, they kept walking on the sidewalk...the same sidewalk they had used to get away from that place. She slowed down even more. Part of her wanted to stop completely. Or maybe to start running in the opposite direction, see if she could break away from the leash. But where could she go?

"What's the matter, Bailey? Is something wrong, girl?"

The woman stopped walking, so Bailey did, too.

"I bet I know. You don't want the walk to be over, do you? I bet it was really nice breathing in all that fresh air. I wish I could walk you longer, but I have a doctor appointment. I need to go home and get ready for it."

The only words Bailey understood were *walk* and *home*. They had definitely been on a walk, but this walk wasn't taking her to this nice woman's home. So, what did she mean? Then a fearful thought took hold...what if the lady was saying that this awful place was Bailey's new home? The lady pulled gently on her leash.

"I'm sorry, Bailey. I wish we could walk longer. But I really have to go. I'll see if I can come back tomorrow, and we can go on another walk."

Reluctantly, Bailey stopped resisting and slowly followed behind the nice lady, accepting her fate.

She was being returned to the awful place. The door was just up ahead.

Kɪᴍ ᴡᴀs in her office just finishing up an email when she heard two quick knocks on the door. She turned to see Angela poking her head inside, her face all smiles.

"Am I interrupting something important?"

"Not really," Kim said. "Come on in and have a seat. I'm just typing out the last sentence on this email to a client. Give me just a sec."

Angela came in and sat down. It was just her and Kim in the office. Amy and Finley had recently left to do a training class.

Kim hit the Send button. "There." She turned around. "I'm all yours. What's up? By the look on your face, I'm guessing it's something I might like."

"It is. Definitely. You'll never guess where Rhonda is, or what she's doing right now?"

"Well, I know she was with Bailey. Is she still?"

"Yes, but they're not in my area anymore. Rhonda's outside, taking her for a walk."

"A walk? She was able to get Bailey on a leash and bring her outside? That's a giant step forward."

"I know, right?" Angela said. "She got her to take a treat, then was able to pet her, so she decided to give it a try. I brought her the leash, and Bailey stood right up and let her put it on. Then off they went. Bailey looked like...well, pretty much like a regular dog."

"Wow, that's great. Maybe she's finally coming out of it."

"Want to come see? They're probably back by now."

"Sure," Kim said. "I can take a few minutes for something like that."

When they got back to the Small Dogs area, Rhonda was indeed back from her walk with Bailey. But something was clearly wrong. Bailey was back in her cage...in the back of her cage, in her full shutdown position. Rhonda was standing nearby, but outside looking in. She looked back at them, when Kim and Angela entered.

"I don't know what happened," Angela said to Kim. They both came closer.

Kim could see the discouragement on Rhonda's face. "Angela came to get me, all excited, because you were able to get Bailey out for a walk."

"We were out for a walk. Just got back. In the beginning, everything was fine. More than fine. Bailey seemed as excited as can be, right up until it was time to head back. I wanted to take her on a longer walk, but I've got to get to the doctors. The closer we got to the building, the slower she walked. I almost had to drag her through the door. When I let her into her pen, it's like she stopped paying attention to me at all. She went right to her old spot, laying like you see her now."

This was discouraging. "I would've loved to see her when she was happy," Kim said.

"What do you think happened?" Angela said.

"Seems obvious to me," Rhonda said. "She doesn't want to be here."

"Yeah," Kim said. "That'd be my guess. Don't think it's any more complicated than that."

"I don't know what to do," Rhonda said. "I can't stay any longer. I can try to get back here tomorrow morning, if you think it'll help."

"That'd be great, if you could," Kim said. "Might help us get her back to at least where she was before the walk. I'd hate to see her go back to square one."

"But aren't we going to need to do something else?" Angela said. "There's no other place for her to go but here. And if we can't get her to start opening up to other people besides Rhonda, she'll never find a new home."

"I know," Kim said, trying to hide her frustration.

"Well," Rhonda said, "I've been thinking...since she was doing so well, really all morning, right up until I started bringing her back here...and you both think it's this place that's the problem...what if I could bring her home to my place for a few days? They talked about that at the orientation meeting. About being a foster home for dogs. Maybe she could come out of her shell more if she was in a home instead of a pen surrounded by all these strange dogs, with all these strange people coming in and out all day."

"That's an idea," Angela said. "What do you think, Kim?"

"There's no way I could keep her permanently," Rhonda said. "But maybe for a few days or a week, just to see if she'd snap out of it."

Kim thought about this. She didn't hate the idea, but it also wasn't as simple as they were making it sound. "Tell you what," Kim said, "let me make a few calls to a couple of our more seasoned foster folks. Really, one in particular. Get his advice. How about I call or email you later this afternoon and we can talk about this some more?"

"That would be great," Rhonda said. "I don't want to give up on this sweet dog." She looked down at Bailey. "Not after we've made so much progress." She glanced at her watch. "I better go. I'll see you tomorrow, Bailey. We'll figure something out."

Bailey made no response.

23

LATER THAT AFTERNOON, KIM WAS DRIVING THE FINAL FEW minutes toward the home of Syd Harper. And yes, they were related. Syd Harper was her father's brother and Kim's favorite uncle. In fact, Uncle Syd was arguably to blame for Kim's dog obsession. He'd never owned less than two in all the years she'd known him. Right now, he was taking care of three. All of them, dogs from Kim's shelter.

Syd Harper was the most experienced and most devoted volunteer in their dogs fostering program. He specialized in taking on older dogs; something most of the volunteers willing to foster dogs were hesitant to do. Because Uncle Syd knew when he took one of them on, it could be for the balance of their life. But he didn't care. He'd take them anyway.

Kim wasn't heading out here to try and talk him into taking Bailey. He'd made it clear...three dogs were his limit. But as she'd told him on the phone when setting up this visit, she just wanted to run the situation by him, see if he'd be willing to meet with her and help evaluate her suggestion about bringing Bailey into her home for a few days.

She turned left off the paved road and drove down the familiar dirt road that led to his property. He and his late wife, Kim's Aunt Sharon, had bought it fifteen years ago when they'd retired. It wasn't a big place. About a half-acre, fenced in, with a modestly-sized three-bedroom house in the center. Uncle Syd and Aunt Sharon got to enjoy the place for ten years together, until cancer had parted their long and happy marriage.

A year later, Uncle Syd ended his long spell of almost overwhelming grief by diving feet-first into the shelter's dog fostering program. "I ain't been lonely a single day since," he'd said many times.

Kim pulled into the driveway and instantly began to hear the three dogs welcoming her from inside the house. She could see each of them in her mind's eye, since she had been much involved with each one before Uncle Syd brought them home. There was Adaline, who was twelve now, a corgi mix. Then Emma, some kind of spaniel mix. She was also twelve. And Evey, the oldest of the three. Kim couldn't remember if she was fourteen or fifteen. She had some terrier in her and a few other things mixed in besides. Evey had been with Uncle Syd the longest.

Even though she was officially listed as still being part of the foster program, everyone knew — at this point — Evey wasn't going anywhere.

The front door opened and out walked Uncle Syd, dressed in his usual outfit: a tropical shirt, khaki shorts, and flip-flops. Like her father, he still had most of his hair, though all of the blonde had gone gray.

"Now you ladies hush," he said. "It's just Kim. I told you she was coming. She'll be in to see you in a minute." He closed the door behind him, but the ladies, if anything, got louder.

"I could help you with that," Kim said as she got out of the car. She was talking about the barking.

"I know you could, but I don't mind them voicing their opinions every now and then. Not like I get a lot of company out here, and we've got enough distance between us that none of the neighbors will complain." He walked toward her. "Really good to see you, Kim. Glad you decided to come out here rather than handle things on the phone."

"Me, too. I was able to get enough done to break free. Besides, I am technically in charge of our foster program, so it's probably a good thing for me to get out here and check up on you every now and then. Make sure you're not ruining these dogs' chances of ever getting adopted."

Uncle Syd laughed. "Well, I hope my setup meets with your approval. Although if it doesn't, at this point might be too far gone to make it right. Come on in and let's get this big greeting over and done with, so we can chat about whatever you came here for."

Then he noticed Kim's ring. She'd wondered how long it would take him.

"What is that? That what I think it is?"

Kim smiled, held her hand out. "It certainly is. Ned finally asked, and I quickly said yes."

"Kim, that's wonderful. I'm so happy for you. For both of you."

They hugged then he led Kim back to the front door. Adeline, Emma, and Evey went absolutely nuts when they saw her. Jumping up and down, running around and just pitching a joyful fit. She squatted down to let them love on her, as she tried to give each one some individual attention. But it was almost impossible, as they each tried to outdo the other in taking center stage. "You three are just awful. You've forgotten everything I've taught you about front door etiquette."

"You can blame me," her uncle said. "They treat me the same way when I get home from the store after a few hours. You'd think I'd traveled around the world for how they carry on. But I do love it so."

"I totally get it," she said, rising to her feet. "Doesn't seem like such a big problem when small dogs do it. So, you won't get any demerits from me."

Syd started walking toward the back porch, so she followed. "Such a nice breeze blowing out there today, thought we'd take advantage of it. Get some fresh air, enjoy the view." He did have a nicely landscaped yard, bordered by a variety of palms and Florida foliage. Something he and Aunt Sharon had worked on together, and he'd done a pretty good job of keeping up with it since she passed.

"Mind if I get some ice water out of the fridge?" Kim said.

"Help yourself. If you need a snack, feel free to rummage around."

"Water's fine. You go on, have a seat. I'll be there in a sec."

Of course, the ladies were all around her, following every move she made. After getting her water, she walked by their water bowl, happy to find it more than half full and looking pretty fresh.

When she got to the porch, Syd said, "Saw you checking the dogs' water bowl. I never forgot that little lesson you gave at the training class on the importance of always keeping their water bowls full and fresh. About how much they need it, and how helpless they are if we forget. Went home and did that homework assignment. Made a lasting impression on me."

Kim had simply asked the class to try going one full day without taking a sip of water. The only exception would be: they could take a drink out of a bowl they had left out in the open the day before.

"So, what's this new situation you've got going on?" he asked. "Something about an older mini Aussie someone dropped off a little while ago."

Kim spent the next fifteen minutes bringing Uncle Syd up to speed on Bailey's situation, including the events of that morning. All the progress they were finally making, then the setback when Rhonda had brought Bailey back to the shelter after her walk. And about Rhonda's suggestion that maybe she should bring Bailey to her house for a few days, see if that might bring her out of this shutdown condition.

"What do you think now that you've got a better understanding of things?"

Uncle Syd sat back in his chair, thought a moment. "So,

what's this Rhonda lady like? From what you said, sounds like the dog's only responding to her so far."

"That's accurate. It's clear Rhonda's developed a heart for Bailey and really wants her to have a chance of finding a new home. And she knows, as we all do —"

"That she has no chance if she doesn't snap out of this... shutdown condition," he said.

"Yep. But Rhonda's also made it clear she can't keep Bailey long-term. We're just trying to evaluate whether this would be a worthwhile experiment."

"Or else something that could backfire, maybe do more harm than good," he said.

"Exactly," Kim said.

"Did Rhonda give any indication why she wasn't open to taking Bailey for more than a few days? Why she couldn't, or wouldn't be able to keep her long-term, as you put it? You know how this fostering thing goes, especially with older dogs. I've been able to see several of them finally get adopted, but it's almost always taken a month or more. Sometimes way more."

"I don't know why, Uncle Syd. Haven't really probed her reasons yet. But I was wondering...would you be open to meeting with her? Let her come out here and talk with you, face-to-face? Think she would benefit a lot more getting with you than me on this."

"I suppose I could do that. She a nice lady? Easy to be with? Easy to talk to?"

Kim smiled. "Yes, yes, and yes. And I'll add to that list... she's a widow. Maybe just a few years younger than you. And I'd say very...well, let's just say she has aged very well."

Uncle Syd smiled. "That's not why I am asking what she's like. I got all the company I need out here from these little ladies." He reached down and stirred up a fuss with Adeline, Emma, and Evey, all sitting around their feet.

"I'm just saying," Kim said, "you could really help us out by meeting with her, and I think you'd enjoy her company."

"Okay then. Go ahead and call her. But get any of those other ideas out of your pretty little head."

24

THE NEXT MORNING, RHONDA HAD DECIDED TO GO BACK TO the shelter and reconnect with Bailey, hoping to at least get her back to where she was before yesterday's walk. Connie, Rhonda's next-door neighbor, was all better. So, they rode in together, since it was Connie's regularly scheduled morning to volunteer. They had just pulled into the shelter parking lot. On the drive over, Rhonda had filled her in on all of her adventures with Bailey.

"So, do you think you're going to try to take her out for another walk?" Connie said. "That's what I'll be doing. I can keep an eye out for you."

"I don't think so," Rhonda said. "Unless Angela or Kim want me to. Her reaction when I started to bring her back was really bad. On the first part of the walk, she went from being as happy and carefree as any normal dog to one of instant and total depression. I left her all curled up in the back of her cage, looking away, like she had been doing for days."

"So, what are you going to do with her?"

Rhonda sighed. "Try to rebuild the bridge somehow. Kim sent me a text yesterday afternoon, asking for me to stop in and see her if I was coming in today. She probably wants to talk about the idea of me taking Bailey home for a few days."

"You going to get involved with the foster care program?" Connie said.

"I don't know. I guess if I have to. I'm really only thinking of it as an experiment, something we can try for a few days. I'm wondering if we can get Bailey in a home environment — even though it's not the home she's used to — it might help her snap out of this thing. It's got to be better than sitting alone in that dog pen day in and day out all by herself."

Connie turned the car off, and they both got out. "You can go on in, start your dog walking adventure," Rhonda said. "I think I'll go into the office, talk with Kim before going to visit Bailey. She said it wouldn't take long, so I'll probably see you in the dog room when you're done with your walk. I'll just be sitting there visiting with Bailey."

"Okay, hope everything works out." Connie headed toward the Small Dog room.

A FEW MINUTES LATER, Rhonda was standing in front of Kim's office door. She knocked and heard a different woman's voice say come in. She opened it and was quickly greeted by a big lovable golden retriever. Kim and this other young lady sitting in another desk turned to greet her.

"Who do we have here?" Rhonda said, patting the dog's head. "Such a handsome boy, and so polite." The dog just sat there wagging his tail and gazing up at her adoringly. He didn't jump or bark.

"That's Finley. He's mine. Well, mine and my husband's. I'm Amy, the assistant dog trainer out here." She held out her hand and Rhonda shook it.

"Nice to meet you both." She turned to Kim. "You said to stop in and see you if I came in."

"That's right, I did." Kim turned around and picked a slip of paper off her desk. "Got something for you." She handed it to Rhonda.

It was a man's name and phone number. "Syd Harper," Rhonda said. "Any relation?"

"He's my uncle. My favorite uncle to be more precise. But he also happens to be our very best and most experienced foster dog parent. He's taking care of three at the moment. I was out to see him yesterday afternoon and we talked about Bailey, and the suggestion you had about taking her home for a few days. He said he'd be willing to meet with you out at his place sometime today. Or, some other time if today won't work out. He's retired, so his schedule's pretty flexible."

"Like mine," Rhonda said. "I'd definitely like to speak with him. I could go right out there now, after I'm done meeting with Bailey, if he's up for that. I'll need his address. Never figured out how to use the GPS gizmo in my car, but I did get my phone GPS to work."

"Okay," Kim said. "Let me have that back, and I'll write the address on the back." When finished, she handed it back to Rhonda. "So, what are you thinking about Bailey? About what you're hoping to accomplish this morning?"

"Well, I figured I'd ask you if you had any advice. I was just gonna spend some time with her, see if I could rebuild some trust. I wasn't even thinking about sitting in her cage like before. Maybe just sit in a chair outside and talk to her, see how she responds to that."

"You have pretty good instincts, Rhonda. That's exactly what I was going to suggest. But I don't think you should feel like you've lost her trust. I thought about what happened a little last night. About why she reacted so dramatically to being brought back to her pen. Sometimes we forget that they can't understand most of what we're saying, so when we talk about doing things for them with the best of intentions, they don't have any idea what we're up to. My guess is, all that progress you made was real. Bailey really was beginning to accept you and let you into her world. I think she might have actually thought when you took her for a walk, you were taking her out of this place for good and bringing her home. Then when you turned around and started heading back here, she suddenly realized that wasn't true."

"Which totally explains her instant depression," Rhonda said. "So, if that's true, do you think it might be a bad idea, this plan to bring her home for a few days to my place? Won't that just reinforce the idea that this is something permanent, and then ruin her completely when I bring her back?"

Kim didn't immediately reply. She looked over at Amy, who made a face like she thought it might.

"Do you think it could backfire?" Kim asked Amy.

"I don't know," Amy said. "After hearing this whole thing through, I think it could. So hard to say."

Kim looked back at Rhonda. "I know, run that by my uncle. See what he thinks."

"Good," Rhonda said. "That's what I'll do then. I'll call him now just to set up a time, then go visit Bailey for a little while."

Rhonda left the office and stepped outside to call this Uncle Syd fellow. She got his voicemail, so she left a message saying she could come out there in an hour or so, or sometime later today if he'd rather her do that. Then she headed into the Small Dog room and found Bailey, as expected, laying in the back of her cage.

Rhonda began to brief Angela on the recent developments when something pretty wonderful happened. Bailey heard Rhonda talking. She lifted her head, turned, and started wagging her little tail. Then she stood up and walked to the front of her cage looking right at Rhonda.

"My goodness," Angela said. "Would you look at that?"

It warmed Rhonda's heart.

"Guess all is forgiven," Angela said. "Not that you did anything wrong."

"I know what you mean."

Just then an older couple came in looking to adopt a small dog. They were all smiles and seemed very pleasant but Bailey instantly retreated to the back of her pen and curled up in her familiar little ball.

Rhonda decided to wait until the couple left before continuing her visit with Bailey. She was encouraged to see how Bailey responded to her moments ago, but seeing how she reacted to the couple made her realize...they still had so very far to go before Bailey could ever find her forever home.

25

AFTER RHONDA HAD A NICE VISIT WITH BAILEY, STILL STAYING on the outside of the cage, Connie had come in from her scheduled dog walking session. Rhonda had tried to introduce Connie to Bailey, but Bailey wasn't quite up for it. She quickly moved to the back of a pen and curled up in a ball. At least, she didn't look away this time as she used to do. But nothing Rhonda had said could coax her into greeting Connie.

"I know I need to get you home," Rhonda said. "And I know this doesn't look like much, but you should've seen her a little while ago."

"Oh, I believe you," Connie said. "I'm not offended. She's just not ready to widen her circle beyond you."

Rhonda said her goodbyes to Bailey and Angela, and they headed for the car.

When they got inside, Connie said, "You are really getting pretty serious about this stuff."

"Why do you say that?"

"I heard you tell Bailey you'd be back again tomorrow to see her. Won't that be four days in a row?"

"It will. And it gets worse than that."

"What do you mean?"

"After I drop you off back at the house, I'm headed to another shelter-related appointment on the edge of town."

"Really? What's that about?"

Rhonda told her about meeting Kim's uncle, Syd Harper, to discuss the idea of bringing Bailey to Rhonda's house for a few days, see what he thought about the experiment. He'd gotten back with her a short while ago.

"So, now you're thinking of bringing Bailey to your place? Wow, Rhonda, I think it's fair to say your dog devotion has just leaped way ahead of mine. You sure you want to do that? That's quite a commitment."

"I'm just thinking of a few days, nothing permanent. Just to see if it snaps her out of this problem she's having with people. I'm wondering if it's more because of that place and what it represents to her. The fact that she can be almost normal around me now makes me wonder if she wasn't in that pen, and she had a chance to be free of it for several days, maybe she could return to her normal personality."

"So," Connie said, "that's why you're meeting with Kim's uncle? I think I know Syd from some of the volunteer meetings. Not well. But he seems like a nice man. Think he's a widower, not that you're out shopping for a companion."

"I'm definitely not," Rhonda said. "This is just to learn what I can about caring for an older dog that isn't yours."

The rest of the time was spent chatting about Connie's

adventures that morning walking three different dogs. Rhonda dropped her off at her place, then keyed in the address of Kim's uncle into the GPS app on her phone.

It was only fifteen minutes away.

After a pleasant drive beyond the town out to the more rural area of Summerville, Rhonda was soon informed by the GPS lady that her destination was just up ahead on the left. Sure enough, she found the mailbox out by the driveway with the correct street number, bearing Mr. Harper's name, right where it was supposed to be. After pulling into the driveway and stopping her car, she turned off her phone and put it back in her purse.

She was quite pleased with herself, not that she had made it here uneventfully, but that she had done so using this amazing phone. It was still such a peculiar thing to her, all the things it could do. Like this. Perfectly directing her from her little home all the way out here to a part of town she had never been to before...without making a single wrong turn.

Ted would have been so proud. For the entirety of their marriage, he was the navigator. He bore the sole responsibility of getting them to places without getting lost. Not that he always succeeded, but he made sure they got there — wherever they were going — one way or the other. She'd never had to give it a thought.

It was one of the many things that had made her feel so utterly helpless when he'd died so suddenly. How would she ever get around town, beyond those few places she knew well? Her son was the one who had insisted she upgrade her phone, took her down to the phone store, picked it out and then showed her how to use the GPS app.

Now look at her. She could drive anywhere.

Her thoughts were interrupted by the front door of the house opening up. Out ran three small, excited dogs followed by a man who must be Syd Harper. He looked at her, smiled, and waved. He was a little taller than Ted, a little thinner, and appeared to be at least a few years older. He had way more hair, but it was grayer and parted on the opposite side. Like Ted, he had a nice smile that he obviously used often, and kind eyes.

Then she realized what she was doing. Comparing him to Ted. Why had she done that? She never compared men to Ted. Then she realized why she was. Had to be what Connie had said on the ride home, about knowing Syd being a nice man and a widower. Then adding, *Not that you're shopping around for a companion.*

That's right. She most certainly was not.

"You must be Rhonda," Syd said, as he came closer. "All right ladies, let's quiet down and be nice."

The dogs actually stopped barking. Rhonda opened her door. "As excited as they were, I noticed they weren't jumping up on the car."

"That's Kim's doing. She trained them on that one. And pretty much anything else you see them doing that might impress you."

"And look how quickly they stopped barking when you told them to."

"I'm about as surprised at that as you are. Can only get them to do that about half the time."

"I'm Rhonda," she said, holding out her hand. "Thanks so much for being willing to get with me, especially on such short notice."

"Pleased to meet you, Rhonda. And happy to spend the time. Always nice to talk to one of God's creatures who talks back."

Rhonda laughed.

"My ladies here are great listeners, but every conversation pretty much ends the same way. Well, let's go on in the house."

She followed him back inside, the three little dogs circling around her feet, just far enough away not to trip her up.

"They'll probably give you some peace if you take a few moments and interact with them. After that, they usually settle down pretty good. Want some coffee? Was going to make a fresh pot."

"I'd love some."

"Half-caff okay?"

"What I usually drink at home," she said. "You wouldn't have any half-and-half, would you?"

"I would. It's not coffee without it." He smiled. "You go in and get acquainted with the girls." He pointed to the living room. "I'll get the coffee together and join you in a moment. Oh, almost forgot to make the introductions. That spaniel mix who can't seem to get enough of you is Emma. The corgi mix is Adaline. They're both twelve. And the terrier mix is the oldest. That's Evey. She's been with me the longest."

Rhonda walked into the living room and bent down to

get closer to the three dogs. They eagerly responded. "Nice to meet you ladies. You're such good dogs." The more she pet them, the happier they got. She'd almost forgotten...this was how healthy dogs reacted to human kindness and attention. And this is what she wanted Bailey to be like, even to a relative stranger.

A few minutes later, Syd came back holding a tray with two mugs and fixings for coffee. "How about we meet outside on the patio instead of in here? It's such a nice cool day. Won't be too long before the heat and humidity start showing up again, forcing us all to live indoors."

"I'd like that," she said. "That's definitely one thing my husband, Ted, used to say about Florida. If it weren't for air conditioning being widely available and affordable, there'd be a mass exodus up north."

"I'd have to agree with him on that," Syd said. "Kim told me you're a widow, like me. Only a widower, guess they call us. How long have you been on your own?" They made it out to the patio. Syd set the coffee tray on a table.

"Just over six years," Rhonda said. "I'm mostly used to it now, but it took me a long while. We'd been together since just after high school, and he died suddenly. A heart attack. Gone just like that. My whole world went...well, I'm sure you understand."

Syd began to fix his coffee. "I definitely do. Been five years since I lost Sharon. Had a little more time to prepare for it than you did, but I was still nowhere near ready when it happened. Took me several years to feel anything close to normal, too. We'd been together since high school. Part of the reason I got involved with these gals here, to combat the loneliness."

"Looks like they keep you pretty busy," Rhonda said, mostly to change the subject. Although in some ways, it felt refreshing to talk with someone who had also lost the great love of their life after being together so long. Then she realized, she'd had some conversations like this but, up until now, they had always been with other widows like her.

Never with a man.

"So," Syd said, sipping his coffee, leaning forward just a little. "Tell me about Bailey. This little dog you been trying to help out down at the shelter."

This guy, Syd, she thought...really did have the kindest eyes.

26

RHONDA SPENT THE NEXT FIFTEEN MINUTES UPDATING SYD ON her experiences with Bailey thus far. He didn't offer any advice as she spoke but asked a lot of good questions. It was obvious, he really wanted to understand what was going on. While they talked, his three dogs napped. When she thought she'd explained enough, she said, "So, what do you think?"

"I agree, it's a tricky situation. Of course, I'm well acquainted with the challenges of trying to re-home an older dog. Can't say I've experienced anything quite as intense as that shutdown condition you described with the older dogs I've dealt with. Most go through a few days of depression, which is understandable, but nothing as dramatic as what Bailey seems to be wrestling with. I commend you for your patience with her. Don't think too many people would've kept at it the way you have, given how long it's been going on."

"Well, thanks," Rhonda said. "Not sure I can explain it, but the more time I spend with her, the more I want to see her pull through this. As I said, there has been some real progress with Bailey."

"It's just that it's all been connected to you," Syd said. "And you're hoping she starts acting that way with other people."

"That's right. Otherwise, she'll never get adopted. Except for me, she shows no interest in people who come by her cage. Doesn't even look at them."

Syd leaned back in his chair. "Yeah, not likely to attract anybody behaving like that. And you think bringing her to your place for a few days might make a difference. Explain to me again how."

"Well, I'm assuming by how she's acting that her depression is tied to being in that cage all day. That, and of course, being torn away after so many years from the owner she loved. That part can't be helped. But seeing how well she is responding to me shows me she is open to the idea of caring about someone else. When we were on that walk, she was acting as normal as can be. Right up until the time I started heading back to the shelter. I'm thinking if she can just be with someone she does feel comfortable with, in a home environment for several days in a row, it will reawaken her interest in people, in general. Not just in me. Does that make any sense?"

"Makes plenty of sense," Syd said. "As an idea, or a concept. There's just no way of knowing if that's how it will play out. She might do what you're saying. Have you thought about what you'll do if Bailey doesn't respond the way you're thinking?"

"No, not really. Guess, I'm just hoping she will. Haven't thought through a Plan B yet."

"I also noticed," Syd said, "that you're using the timeline of a few days. Meaning, you'll bring her home for a few days to see if that will do the trick. Can I ask what's behind that?"

"Just thinking that we should be able to see by then if she's acting like a normal dog. You know, all day long without returning to that shutdown condition. Do you think that's unrealistic?"

He sipped his coffee again. "No, based on what you said, I can easily see Bailey come around in that length of time. You might get to see the kind of dog she used to be in her previous life. But I can also just as easily see her returning to her shutdown state — as you call it — within hours of being brought back to the shelter. I think all the confusion she's been grappling with since being dropped off there the first time would all come rushing back."

Rhonda's heart sank hearing this.

Syd could tell. "I'm not trying to discourage you, but you were looking for my advice, right? Not saying that would happen for sure, I'm just saying —"

"No, you don't need to apologize. I guess I've thought about that very thing but wouldn't let myself acknowledge it. Do you think that's more likely how she'll react? Or just a slim chance she will."

Syd didn't immediately reply, which Rhonda took to mean he did think it more likely she'd react poorly. "So, what should I do? Seems like if I take her home and she does come out of it, only to send her right back to the way she is now, I'm not helping any. Maybe making things worse."

Syd sighed. "It's a tough one. I'll give you that. But I can think of one solution to your dilemma. But it would involve a bit more sacrifice on your part. And I won't judge you if you decide you're not up for it."

"What are you thinking? Whatever it is, I want to hear it."

"Well, it would involve you pretty much doing the plan you described, except letting go of the...*for a few days* part. See, what you're suggesting isn't something they normally do at the shelter. You're not really talking about becoming part of the foster care program. Because that involves taking a dog home and caring for it there, rather than at the shelter, while we wait for someone to adopt it. That involves a considerably longer commitment. Could be a few weeks. Could be a few months. I've had it go both ways. But never just a few days. Especially with older dogs."

"Oh," she said.

"Both Adeline and Emma have been with me a couple of months each. And Evey, well, I've had her for over a year. Technically, all three are still listed as adoptable through the shelter. They're on the website and everything. I still have hope that Adeline and Emma will still find a permanent home. But I think old Evey here is already in the last home she'll ever know. And I'm okay with that."

"I see," Rhonda said. "Has anyone come out to look at any of these dogs? You know, people who are considering adopting them?"

"Yeah, a few. But just for Adeline and Emma. Two different people each. No takers yet. But see, the nice part of it is, while we're waiting they're enjoying life right here. They're not stuck in a pen down at the shelter. See, if you would decide to become Bailey's foster parent, there is no chance she'd return to that sad, shutdown condition. People would pick her out from her picture on the website, make an appointment with you to see her, and what they'd see is a happy, healthy Bailey who's temporarily living with you. I can pretty much guarantee from the success stories I've had, although she might experience some confusion transferring from you to someone else, it would be nothing like the traumatic thing she just went through."

"I can definitely see that." Now, she sighed. "Can I ask you something somewhat related, but not quite? About why you decided to care for older dogs in the first place? That's what Kim told me."

"That's correct. All the dogs I've fostered for the shelter were ten years or older. Evey's been my oldest, at fourteen."

"How do you deal with...well, I guess the built-in sadness of the situation? What I mean is, taking on and getting deeply attached to a dog that only has a few years left? I really miss my Amos, but I just can't see me ever getting another dog. I was so heartbroken when he died. It was almost — though not quite — as devastating as when Ted died. I was depressed for weeks, maybe even a few months. But at least I had Amos for almost 15 years. I can't imagine volunteering for all that heartache, taking on a dog that's already just a few years away from the end."

Syd shook his head, as if agreeing with her. "Those are

good points, Rhonda. I hear what you're saying. What I'm doing is certainly not for everybody. But my wife Sharon and I had four dogs during the years we were together. And we stayed true to each one of them from their first days as a pup until their journey on this earth was through. As hard as it was to let them go—and believe me, it was plenty hard —I knew it was the right thing to do."

"I had Amos the same way, too...from a pup all the way to the end," she said.

"That's something all dog lovers must face," Syd said, "the reality of the lifespan God's set for them. Seems way too short for us, especially compared to the depth of love and joy they bring to the relationship. But staying with them through to the end—as painful as that moment is— it's the last, final way for us to thank them for all that joy they gave. So, they don't have to face that moment alone. Instead of being afraid, their last moments are spent gazing into the face of someone they love, someone they know loves them."

Rhonda suddenly got choked up, felt tears welling up in her eyes. She saw Syd was getting teary-eyed, too. He blinked them away.

"Now, take a dog like old Evey here," he continued. "Like most of the older dogs that get brought to the shelter, something happened to keep them from being able to end their journey with the people they started out with. Nothing they did wrong. It just happened. The way I see it, they still deserve to spend their final years with someone who loves them and will be there for them when that time comes. I consider it a privilege to be that someone. Believe me, even though she didn't start the first part of her life with me, old Evey here loves me and cares about me like nobody's business. Dogs have a capacity to love their owners that, to me, almost defies comprehension. So, I just decided the heartbreak I'm gonna feel when her time comes...well, it's a small price to pay to thank her for all the love she's given to me. So, hard as it'll likely be...I will be there for her."

Tears slid down Rhonda's cheeks. "Now, look what you've done to me," she said. "You have a napkin I can use?"

"I'm sorry," Syd said, getting up. "Didn't mean to make you sad."

"You didn't make me sad. That was...well, the sweetest thing I've heard anyone say in a long while. And you've given me a whole lot to think about, Syd. That's for sure."

27

When Rhonda pulled into her driveway, she saw Connie doing some weeding in her front beds. Connie waved but then kept on waving. She wanted Rhonda to come over and chat. Rhonda preferred to go in the house, have some time alone to think and pray about all the things she and Syd had talked about. But she got out of the car and walked across the yard toward Connie.

"I was hoping I'd see you when you got back," Connie yelled. "Wanted to hear how your time went with Syd. He help you sort out your plans about Bailey?"

Rhonda waited to respond until she got a little closer. No sense broadcasting her plans to everyone nearby. "It went very well. Better than I expected. Well, that's not exactly what I mean. I didn't go there with low expectations. What I meant was, I came back with a lot more than I bargained for."

Connie stood up, took off her garden gloves. "Not sure

how to take that, but it sounds like a good thing the way you said it."

"It is a good thing. Learned a good bit from our chat. He's an easy man to be with."

"Oh my," Connie said, "that sounds interesting."

"No, I meant...as in easy to talk with. You know what I mean. Some men don't have much to say, others have too much. Makes conversation difficult. Syd had it just about right."

"Had it just about right," Connie repeated. "That's a good quality in a man, in terms of conversation I mean. So, what kind of things did you learn?"

"Well, he's fostering three dogs at the moment. And all three are older than Bailey. He's had two of them for a few months, one quite a bit longer. But here's the thing, although their relationship is relatively new, you wouldn't know it seeing how the three dogs interact with him. They seem as happy and secure as dogs who'd been living with him their whole lives. Did my heart good to see that. Gave me hope that Bailey could come fully out of this doggy depression if I brought her home with me. Which means, when people interested in adopting her want to see her, they'll see her as she really is, not the way she looks now."

"That's definitely a good thing," Connie said. "Sounds like you've decided to do it, then."

"I think I have, but there's something else along these lines that Syd gently challenged me on."

"And what's that?" Connie asked.

Rhonda hesitated to say. Even as she thought about it, she realized it was such a greater sacrifice than the one she'd planned on making. She went on to explain how Syd fully believed Bailey would quickly bounce back to her normal self within a few days of living with her. But he wasn't sure this bouncing back situation would stick. He could easily see her returning to her shutdown state within twenty-four hours of being brought back to the shelter."

Connie nodded her head. "I can see that, too. In fact, when you first explained to me your idea that thought occurred to me, but I didn't want to say anything discouraging."

"Well, the way Syd handled it, I wasn't discouraged. But it was kind of a reality check. The whole reason I'm doing this is to help Bailey, not to give her a few days off from her suffering, only to bring her right back to it."

"So, what did Syd suggest you do instead?"

"Well, that's just it. The only thing I can do...is to become a regular foster care volunteer. And then bring Bailey here for as long as it takes."

"Until she gets adopted, you mean."

"Yes. It could take a few weeks, maybe even a few months. That's been Syd's experience. He's been doing it for three years."

"Are you up for that? That's kind of a big leap from volunteering to walk dogs three times a week, like I do, to taking one home for such a long time."

"I know," Rhonda said. "If you had told me a couple weeks ago that I'd be considering such a thing, I'd have said you're crazy. But here I am. That's what I'm planning to do." She looked at her watch. "Guess there's still time to call Kim at the shelter and see what she thinks of all this."

"I can't see her having a problem with it," Connie said. "They're always talking about needing more volunteers for the foster care program. So, once this happens, if people want to see Bailey do they come here, or do you meet them at the shelter?"

"I hope we can meet here, or maybe at some park. I think once Bailey gets away from that place, she's not gonna ever want to see it again."

Connie laughed. "Probably be like how my dog used to be about the vet. She'd start whining and shaking the moment we pulled into the parking lot."

"That's exactly how Amos used to be," Rhonda said. "Anyway, I'm sure I'll find out all the details when I talk to Kim."

"Before you head back into the house," Connie said, "you mentioned something about a reality check a few moments ago. Since I didn't speak up on this one before, maybe I should mention another one I started thinking about while you were explaining this new idea. Mind if I share it?"

"No, not at all."

"Have you thought about...what I mean is, this idea of taking Bailey into your home for the long haul. You know, until she gets adopted. Have you thought about the effect that can have on you? Seems to me, you're really going out of your way for this dog. Which is a good thing. Don't get me wrong. But it shows a level of bonding toward her that's already going on inside you. I can only imagine once she's here and really starts to come alive, and the two of you start clicking... It's going to be extremely hard for you to let her go and live the rest of her life with someone else. Don't you think?"

"No," Rhonda said. "I appreciate your concern. But there's no way I want to get involved in a permanent situation. I'm looking at this more like, if this thing with Bailey works out, maybe I want to do something like Syd. You know, be more of a foster care volunteer to other dogs after she's in a new home. I'm sure when the time comes it'll be a little challenging, but I'm keeping my heart in my chest on this. I'm not sure I'll ever want to get a dog permanently again. Not at my age."

"Okay. Just checking. Mind if I share one more thing? Not a reality check. More of an...observation."

"Sure," Rhonda said.

"You seem to be a little taken with Syd. Unless I'm reading this wrong. Ever since I've known you, and since your husband passed, I've never seen you show even a little bit of interest in a man. Any man. But there's this gleam in your eye when you talk about Syd —"

Rhonda laughed. "Oh, no, Connie. You're definitely reading this wrong. Spending too much time watching those Hallmark movies. I did enjoy meeting with Syd, and talking with him really helped. But what you're hearing? It's just respect. That's all."

"Okay then," Connie said. "I'll let it go. Let me know what Kim says about this and when you're going to be bringing that little doggy home."

"I will," Rhonda said. "We'll talk soon."

28

WHEN RHONDA WALKED INTO HER HOME, SHE CAME THROUGH the side door which led into the kitchen. Without thinking, she looked down at the floor beside the first cabinet and could easily remember seeing Amos there eating his dinner or drinking some water. That's where she'd kept his bowls. He'd always make such a mess. But after he'd died, she sure missed cleaning it up. Hard to imagine she was about to let another little dog live in her house.

She poured herself a glass of ice water, sat down at the dinette table, and picked up her phone. She tapped the button for Kim's number and was surprised to hear her voice after three rings.

"Hello, this is Kim Harper at the Humane Society. How can I help you?"

"Hi, Kim. Expected to get your voicemail. This is Rhonda, and you've already been a great help. Got home a little while ago after having a nice visit with your Uncle Syd."

"Well, hi Rhonda. I'm glad you had a nice time. He's one of my favorite people."

"I can see why. He was very easy to talk with, and very helpful."

"I'm glad to hear that. Did he have any good ideas or suggestions about what to do with Bailey?"

"He did. Actually, that's why I'm calling. To give you an update but also to follow-up on one of the big things we discussed."

"I appreciate that. I'm all ears."

Rhonda spent the next ten minutes summarizing the things she'd talked about with Syd leading up to the final item...that is, Rhonda agreeing to take Bailey into her home as a regular foster care situation, not just for a few days as an experiment.

"Just to be clear, Rhonda, you didn't feel any pressure from Uncle Syd to do this, did you? I know he's pretty passionate about this idea. I hope you didn't feel manipulated in —"

"Oh, no, Kim. I didn't feel any pressure at all. In fact, your uncle handled the situation very gently. He asked me a lot of questions and let me say whatever I had to say. The more we talked, the more I realized my idea wouldn't really work. I mean, not the first part. We both agreed Bailey would snap out of this state she's been in shortly after coming into my home. But I could also see all that progress going out the window as soon as I brought her back to the shelter."

"I see. Can't say I disagree with that. So you're thinking of taking her in as a regular foster parent then? I know that sounds a little silly, saying *parent*. But you know what I mean."

"I do," Rhonda said. "And I don't mind the term. But yes, that's the plan now. If you're okay with it, I'd like to bring her here for as long as it takes to find her a permanent home."

"Did my uncle explain how long it could take? What his experience has been?"

"He did. He was very upfront with me. And I appreciated that. So, I'm going into this with my eyes wide open."

"Good, I'm glad. Did he explain to you what's involved in fostering Bailey versus the idea you had?"

"No, we didn't get that far. He was more or less just introducing the idea to me, something he thought I might want to think about. Of course, that's what I did, which led me to the conclusion that fostering Bailey is the real solution to this dilemma. So, where do we go from here?"

"Well," Kim said, "it's fairly simple. You just have to take our two-hour foster care class, very similar to the orientation class you've already taken. We'll likely have less people attending. And it just so happens, our next one is already on the calendar. Two Saturdays from now, between ten and noon."

"Do you teach it or someone else?"

"Like the orientation class, I teach part of it and — as it happens — my Uncle Syd teaches part of it. He's also there for the Q&A at the end, since he has so much more experience than I do at fostering dogs."

"Oh, that's nice," Rhonda said. She meant that Syd was involved, but quickly added, "that you and your uncle get to do it together."

"It is. So, would you like me to sign you up?"

"Definitely. I'm writing the information down now. Is this class the only thing required to qualify to do this?"

"That and making sure you've gotten any permission that might be needed to bring a dog into your home. I'm pretty sure your community allows one or two small dogs, don't they?"

"They definitely do. Had a dog named Amos for several years here, until he died. And I see people walking their dogs all the time."

"Then you should be all set."

"Does that mean I take Bailey home with me after the class?"

"I don't see why not," Kim said. "We have a checklist of things a foster parent should get for their dog before they bring it home. Usually give it out at the meeting, but I'll email it to you when we get off the phone, so you can be all set right after the meeting."

"That would be great, Kim. Thank you. And if it's okay, I'll plan to come down every morning to visit Bailey, except maybe Sunday's, between now and the class."

"That would be wonderful, if you could," Kim said. "I'm sure Bailey will like that, too. Well, my other line is ringing, so I better go."

"That's okay. We'll talk soon." Rhonda hung up, walked over to her calendar, and wrote down the date and time for the meeting. Without intending to, she found herself especially looking forward to seeing Kim's Uncle Syd again so soon.

KIM WAS LOVING how this Bailey situation was developing. She picked up her phone and dialed Angela's extension in the Small Dog room. After Angela answered, Kim spent a few moments updating her on Rhonda's decision about Bailey.

"That's wonderful," Angela said. "I'm sure that will help a lot. So, she'll start coming to see her every morning starting tomorrow?"

"That's what she said. And every day except Sunday until the class two Saturdays from now. And listen, if between now and then anyone expresses an interest in adopting Bailey, that takes priority. We don't want to act like this plan is in granite. The whole reason we're going this way is to —"

"Don't mean to interrupt you, Kim, but I don't think you have to worry about that. Even now, Bailey is laying there like she always does curled up in the back of her cage. Nobody has taken enough interest to even ask to see her. I don't think there's any chance of Bailey getting adopted between now and the class."

"Okay, you're probably right. I've got to go. Just wanted to give you the good news."

She hung up then decided there was one more person she needed to call...her Uncle Syd. She found his number and tapped the screen. A few rings later, he answered.

"How's my favorite uncle doing?"

"I'm doing pretty good," he said. "Got all my chores done early, so now I can just relax, put my feet up, and be retired."

"That's good, I'm glad. Thought I'd call and say thanks again for being willing to meet with Rhonda today. Sounds like the meeting was a big hit."

"I guess you spoke with her," Uncle Syd said.

"I did. Just a little while ago. She sounded very upbeat about your time together. She called to update me but also to inform me she's decided to become Bailey's foster parent and wanted to know what she had to do to make that happen."

"She did? Well, isn't that a nice thing? I'm so glad. You sure she seemed fine about it? I hoped I wasn't laying it on too thick."

"I'm sure you weren't. In fact, I kind of asked that question just to make sure, and she assured me she felt absolutely no pressure from you. Even said she thought you handled the situation very gently."

"Good," he said. "I'm so glad. That means she's signing up for the class?"

"Already signed up. And I already emailed her that sheet we hand out. You know, that checklist of things to get for the dog before bringing it home."

"Good. I think she's going to have a really easy time of it. She's got a very calm demeanor, which dogs love as you know. And she is clearly very dedicated to this dog."

"She also had some very nice things to say about you."

"She did? Like what?"

"Like how smart you are, and wise...and how handsome."

"She didn't say that."

"Not the last part, no. But I know she was thinking it. How could she not? You are handsome."

"Now you're being silly," Uncle Syd said. "But I guess if I'm being honest, I'll be looking forward to seeing her again...two Saturdays from now."

29

As Kim was leaving work, Ned surprised her in the parking lot. She thought he was working today, but there he was driving his regular car and wearing regular clothes. "What's going on? I mean, I'm always happy to see you, but...is everything okay?"

"Everything's great," he said through the open window. "Thought I'd take a chance that you'd be getting off, since you often finish up around the same time. How about I take you out for dinner? Nothing fancy, like Villa de Palma. Actually, thinking of a place almost at the opposite end of the spectrum. In the mood for Italian?"

"Sorrento's?" she said.

"That's what I was thinking."

They had been there a number of times before. "Sure. You know I love the food there, and I know you love the price."

He smiled. "Great. Hop in. I'll bring you back to your car after."

She came around the front and got in the passenger door. They kissed and she said, "Is this just for fun, or is there something you wanted to talk about?"

"Well, I hope you'll think it's fun, but I did have something I thought we should talk over. If you're okay with it, I'd like to make some wedding plans."

"You would?"

"Yes," he said.

THIRTY MINUTES LATER, they were sitting at their favorite table at Sorrento's. The waitress had just brought their iced teas and taken their order. They didn't need to look at the menus. Ned and Kim shared the culinary trait of always ordering the same thing when returning to a favorite restaurant. As Ned put it, "*That's why I come to this place, for the...*" At Sorrento's, what came next was always baked ziti with meatballs. For Kim it was linguine with white clam sauce. Not only was the food great, but they could both eat for about the price of the tip they'd left for their waiter at Villa de Palma.

"Okay," Ned said. "Guess I'll start things off. What motivated me doing this now was, I'm hoping the outcome of our little chat here will mean we can get married sooner, than later. I know we've talked about not waiting too long, but that's too vague for me. I'd like to see if you're open to the idea of picking a date that's only as far off as it needs to be to get everything done that you want done for the wedding. Does that make sense?"

Kim smiled. "There's a lot there, but it actually does."

"I mean," he continued, "I know we both have friends and family who'd want us to have a real wedding with all the fixings. So, I'm not trying to rush anything or cut anything out that you want in the wedding. I just thought if we compared notes, maybe we'd find we're not that far off from each other, in terms of what we're hoping for."

"Okay," she said, "let's start with what you're hoping for. Let me get out my tablet."

"No need," he said. "My wish list is very short. Really, just one thing. I want to be married to you as soon as earthly possible. That's it."

She laughed. "That's it?"

"Well, and the other item would be...to make you very happy. I mean, that you get to have the wedding you've always wanted. Let's face it. Most of the traditions and details that go into planning a wedding are because of the ladies and what they want. There are so many bridal magazines and websites and TV shows devoted to weddings. And they're mostly about the brides. I'm okay with that. I'm just hoping that what we wind up doing won't take six months or more."

"Well, Ned. I think you're going to be able to enjoy your ziti and meatballs tonight. Because I have good news. I'm not thinking six months. I'm thinking more like three. Maybe even two, if we can pull it off without going nuts."

A big smile came over his face. "See? That's how I

thought you'd react to what I said. That sounds great to me."

"For starters," she said, "I'm not really thinking of a big wedding. I want it to be special, but that doesn't mean big to me. Since we're quite a few years removed from high school and college, I don't feel the need to invite any of my friends from that era. Most of my friends now are also coworkers at the shelter. Add them to my family members who are likely to come, and we're talking maybe twenty or twenty-five people at most."

"My situation is almost the same," Ned said. "So, fifty people or so. That shouldn't be too hard to manage. And with a number like that, we can invite everyone to the reception after. I'd be happy to pay for some of that, if you or your dad would let me."

"Well, thanks for being willing. Let me talk to my dad, see where he's at on that. I know back when I was in high school he let me know he was putting money every month into a fund for my wedding. Who knows if that money is still in that fund...given how much time has passed."

Ned laughed. "From what I know of your dad, I'll bet it's all still there. But if not, I'm happy to help. I'd really like it if we can have everyone come to the reception who comes to the wedding."

"Me, too."

"Which brings up my next big wedding thing. I know we both want our pastor to do the ceremony, but have you always had your heart set on a church wedding?"

"Well, kind of, sort of. But I'm open on that one. What do you have in mind?"

"Well, anticipating this conversation, I talked with our pastor about scheduling a wedding at the church in the next few months. Sadly, there's a lot going on in the next few months. He said they usually schedule weddings a little further out. So, I did some checking. There are several really nice parks in and around town that are set up to have outdoor weddings. They have quite a few openings in the next few months."

"I'd love an outdoor wedding," Kim said. "Especially, if we can find a place with lots of shade. Shouldn't be too hard to make something like that work with fifty people."

"That would be great, Kim. The pastor said he has several Saturday slots available in the next couple of months, even if the building doesn't."

"Then," she said, "we'll just have to pick the park with the best spot, see what Saturdays it's available, and pick one that works for the pastor."

"You think that's doable in two months or so?" he said.

"Don't see why not."

"What about your wedding dress? Won't that take some time to pick out and order?"

"No. Mom and I will have fun doing that over a few Saturdays. I'm sure I can find something I'll like at one of the local bridal stores. I'm not going to special order anything, or spend a fortune on a dress either."

"That's wonderful," he said. "This is going better than I imagined. I guess the other big planning item is the honeymoon. I've already got some great ideas, and the money is in the bank. I just need to know if there's any way you can get off a week, preferably two, right after the wedding. I checked, and I can do it on my end."

"I already know the answer to that. And it's yes. I've actually got three weeks built up this year, and I haven't used hardly any. As long as I can plan things out for when I'm gone, they won't have a problem with that at work. So, where do you wanna go?"

"Okay if I surprise you?"

"Sure, I guess. Will I need a passport? If so, I'll need time to update mine."

"No, the places I'm thinking about all work with any U.S. ID, like your driver's license. Have you thought about who you're going to ask to be your maid of honor and brides-maids? That can be tricky sometimes, right?"

"I guess it can," she said. "But I don't think it will be for me. I'm just going to ask Amy to be my matron of honor, and with such a small wedding, I don't think we need to have any bridesmaids or ushers, do you?"

"Nope. Works for me."

"Who are you going to ask to be your best man?" She really had no idea who he might ask. So far, while he did have a lot of friends at work, none seemed to fit the best friend category.

"I was thinking...Parker? You know, he's kind of the one who brought us together."

"Parker? Your dog?" This was absurd.

"Yeah, don't you think that would be cool? A dog is man's best friend. Why can't he be man's best man?"

She didn't know what to say.

He burst out laughing. "I'm not going to ask Parker. I'm totally kidding."

She exhaled a sigh of relief.

"But I was thinking of asking someone who might seem...a little unusual. If you're okay with it."

"Who are you thinking of?"

"My next-door neighbor, Russell. I know he's only ten years old, but I was just thinking—"

"Oh, Ned. Yes. You should do it. Definitely ask Russell. He would be so thrilled."

"You're okay with it?"

"Totally."

Moments later, the waitress walked over carrying a tray filled with the most amazing smelling Italian food.

30

IT WAS SATURDAY. A BIG DAY FOR RHONDA.

She was almost at the Humane Society to attend the orientation class for fostering dogs. After— if no surprises occurred at the class — Rhonda would get to bring Bailey home with her. She had already gone out and bought everything on the list that Bailey would need, including a new dog bed. Kim had said Bailey would probably rather keep the one she's familiar with, but Rhonda thought she'd put that one in the bedroom and put the new one out in the living area.

Before getting in the car, Rhonda had asked her neighbor Connie if she'd like to drive there together. Saturdays were normally one of the days Connie volunteered to walk dogs. But Connie couldn't make it this time. Apparently, she was expecting her new gas stove to be delivered and installed. Rhonda then decided it was probably a good thing that Connie couldn't come today. Might be better for

Bailey if the two of them were alone together on the ride home.

Rhonda pulled into the parking lot and found a space. The shelter was busier on Saturdays than weekdays. Besides the training classes, a lot more people came in to look at dogs. This was close to the time she'd been getting there every day to visit Bailey. Those visits had gone very well. Whenever Rhonda came into the room, Bailey actually got up close to the door of her pen and wagged her little nub. Angela said Rhonda was still the only one who got that kind of treatment. Everyone else still got the cold shoulder. Although Angela did say that with her, Bailey at least now looked up when she talked.

Rhonda decided not to check in with Bailey before heading to class and hoped she wouldn't be sad. But in an hour or two, her whole life was about to change for the better. Rhonda hoped hers was, too.

She found her way to the training classroom. As Kim had said, there were half as many there than had attended the main orientation class. Looking around, she didn't know anyone. Except Kim who was upfront, looking over her notes. Rhonda didn't see any sign of Syd. She was about to ask Kim if he wasn't coming after all but felt that would be showing a little too much interest.

Just as she'd picked out her seat, Syd walked in. His eyes darted around the room until they landed on her. He smiled, nodded, and gave a little wave, then headed to the front and greeted Kim. Rhonda didn't see him acknowledge anyone else and wondered if that was significant, or if she was just reading too much into it. This was unfamiliar territory for her, looking for a certain man in a crowd then finding joy when that man entered and seemed to be looking for her, too.

"Okay, everyone," Kim said. "If I could have your attention, we'll get started. Not expecting any walk-ins for this class, and everyone who signed up is now here. I think most of you know or have met the man standing to my right. If not, this is Syd Harper, my uncle and one of our most seasoned veterans in our dog foster program."

Syd looked around and waved at everyone. "Thanks, Kim. Happy to be here with you all this morning. This is really Kim's class. I'm mostly here to answer any questions you might have about the practical aspects of this program. If I don't know the answer to your question, you'll never know it. I'll just make something up that sounds official."

Everyone laughed, including Kim. "I seriously doubt anyone will ask a question that will stump you, Uncle Syd. Everyone get an outline?" She held one up. Raise your hand if you didn't."

Rhonda and a few others raised their hands. Syd walked around passing them out. After handing Rhonda's to her, he smiled and quietly said, "Glad you could make it."

"Me, too," she whispered back. When he got back to the front, Rhonda noticed he hadn't talked to anyone else. Just her.

Oh, stop it. What are you doing? This isn't high school.

Kim started off by enthusiastically thanking everyone who came, emphasizing how important their foster volunteers are to the success of the shelter. "We have seen case after case where it is abundantly clear, had our foster dog volunteers not been there, countless dogs would have never been placed in a permanent home. Also, every dog that goes to one of your homes frees up a space here in our kennel for another dog to have a chance to be adopted. And it's not just the space situation, but some dogs — for a reason we can't explain — just don't thrive in this environment. But in a home, they can bounce back to become the kind of dog they really are. The kind of dog anyone might love to adopt."

Kim went on to explain a number of different points, each with its own bullet and graphic on a PowerPoint slide. It was very informal and after a brief period, people started asking questions. She talked about the need to either have a fenced-in yard, or be willing to walk the dog on a leash at least twice a day. Even if you have a yard, she said it would be important to still be willing to spend significant time with the dog day to day. The more socializing a shelter dog gets, the better.

Someone asked if any of the dogs needed to be house-trained. Kim said very few needed help with this, since most are older dogs, not puppies. She asked her uncle if he'd ever had a dog that wasn't housebroken. He said no. "But if any of you do run into that situation, Kim here knows how to fix that fairly quick. I'd just give her a call." Then he looked right at Rhonda and smiled.

She looked around but no one seemed to notice it.

Kim went on to cover things like how to handle the food situation. Since most dogs don't crave variety the way people do, she discouraged giving them table scraps. They have all the food the dogs are used to eating here, and the foster program is willing to cover the cost. On the other hand, if people could afford to buy the food themselves, it would be like making a donation to the shelter. Syd added a thought that he sometimes broke this rule and gave them *people food treats*. Of course, he said, "better be prepared for the consequences if your dog has a sensitive stomach."

Once again, he looked right at Rhonda after he spoke. He didn't smile this time, but she had this thought again right after...he has the kindest eyes.

Kim then talked about how they could always bring the dog in to their vet, versus having to spend their own money if a vet was ever needed. And about a half-dozen other things. After, they had about twenty minutes of Q&A. It was all very helpful and informative, though Rhonda had already learned most of it in earlier chats with Kim and Syd.

When the class ended and people began to get up to leave, Syd said something to Kim, who nodded, then he walked right over to Rhonda. "So, you still wanting to do this now that you've heard everything involved?"

"More than ever," she said. "I'm actually going to go pick her up right now and bring her home. I can't wait."

"That's what Kim said. About you picking her up now."

"Thanks again for meeting with me to talk about all this."

"Happy to help. In fact, if you want, I could come over after you pick up Bailey and help you get set up."

"Thanks, but I think I'll be okay. Between the talk we had and this class, I think I'm ready to go."

"I'm sure you'll do great. I bet Bailey's gonna go nuts when you bring her home. That would be a fun sight to see." He turned and started to walk away, then stopped. "Say, listen, once you get settled there with her, you're welcome to bring her over to my place sometime. Might do her good to spend some quality time with some well-adjusted older dogs."

"Thanks for the invitation, Syd. But from what Kim told me, her former owner said she's never been very good with other dogs."

"Oh. That's too bad. Well, anyway, hope you have a real good experience with her."

"Thanks."

"Guess I'll see you sometime then. Maybe at the monthly get-together they have for foster dog parents."

That was one of the things Kim had mentioned in her talk. "I'd like that," Rhonda said. "Definitely planning on going."

"Okay, great," he said. "See you then." He walked back toward the front of the room where Kim was speaking with one of the other attendees.

Rhonda gathered up her things and made her way to the door. It was time to go get Bailey. That was the main reason for the high level of joy she was feeling right now. But it also seemed obvious to her now...Syd's interest in her no longer seemed a figment of her imagination.

She found that this did not bother her one bit.

31

BAILEY WAS STARTING TO GET A LITTLE NERVOUS.

She couldn't be sure, but it felt like the nice lady wasn't coming today. Normally, she'd come while the lady who was here all the time gave out food and changed water bowls. But that lady had finished doing this a while ago. Bailey was pretty sure the nice lady's name was Rhonda. It seemed like the other lady called her that.

Every time the front door opened, Bailey looked up hoping to see Rhonda. So far, it had always been someone else. She'd come to expect her to come every day, spend some time with her, then the other lady would let her redo Bailey's bowls. The entire time she'd talk so nicely to Bailey and pet her. Sometimes, she'd even brush her hair. She didn't take Bailey out for walks anymore. Only that one time. Bailey didn't know why. But she always enjoyed her visits and hoped they didn't stop.

The door opened again. Bailey looked up. It wasn't

Rhonda, just the other lady who worked here bringing in some box. She set it on the table when the door opened again.

It was HER! It was Rhonda! She came back.

Bailey stood up and hurried toward the door of her pen. She couldn't help it. She was just so excited. Rhonda looked over at her and said, "Hello, Bailey," and waved. The other lady started talking to her.

"Today's the big day, right?" Angela said.

"Yes, it is. Just came from the foster class, and we're all set to go. Is there anything else I need to do with you?"

"Nope. Just gather up her things and put her on a leash, and you're free to go."

"Great. I just bought her a new leash and matching collar."

"That's nice," Angela said. "I went ahead and refilled her food bowl and changed her water. Of course, she hasn't eaten any of it yet."

"Well, if it's okay, I'm going to leave those here. Bought her a new matching set of food and water bowls. They're on a nice little stand elevated about eight inches off the ground. Read an article about caring for older dogs. It said they get sore necks and backs just like we do when we age. It recommended elevating their food and water bowls, so they wouldn't have to bend down so far to reach them."

"Sounds like a good idea to me," Angela said. "Let me pour

the food in her bowl back in the bag, so it's not wasted. I've still been using the bag the owner left for her. He said it was her favorite. We don't usually cater to dogs' individual appetites like that. Can't really afford to. But I didn't see any harm letting her eat it, since she wasn't eating very much anyway."

"Is she still not eating well?" Rhonda asked.

"Actually, since you started coming every day she eats a pretty normal amount."

"Well, I got another bag of the food she likes," Rhonda said. "Saw what you were giving her, figured I'd keep it going, since it was her favorite."

"I can tell she's gonna be in great hands."

"I hope she'll like the change."

"Are you kidding? Look at her. She couldn't be more excited. And she only gets this way when she sees you."

"That's because she's my Bailey girl, aren't you?"

Bailey's tail began wagging furiously. "Look," Angela said, "she's actually prancing, she's so excited."

"I'm not sure who's more excited, her or me," Rhonda said.

BAILEY DIDN'T UNDERSTAND much of what they said, but it seemed they were talking about her. Both of them kept looking at her the whole time. And now look, Rhonda was walking this way. And what was she holding in her hand? It looked like...a leash.

"Are you ready to come home with me, girl?" Rhonda said.

Did she say *home*? Bailey knew that word. She must have heard wrong.

Rhonda opened Bailey's door, held out a leash, and said, "Let's put this on, so we can take you *home*."

There it was again. That word. But she was putting Bailey on a leash. Were they going for a walk? Whatever it was, Bailey was so excited she could barely keep still.

"Look at her," Angela said. "I've never seen her like that."

"That's because she's happy," Rhonda said. "Aren't you, girl? You're just happy. Haven't been too happy lately, have you? But that's gonna change, starting today." She clipped on Bailey's leash and led her out of her pen.

"You take care of her," Angela said. "I'll take care of the food and her other things, including the bed. You heading out to your car now?"

"Is that all right?"

"Sure. But I'd walk her in the grass first, so she doesn't have any accidents in the car."

"Good idea. Let's go, girl."

Bailey couldn't believe it. They were walking toward the front door. And the other lady was carrying her bed. Maybe they weren't just going for a walk. Maybe she really did hear the word *home* when they were talking before.

BAILEY COULDN'T BELIEVE IT. Not only had Rhonda taken her for a walk, she'd taken her for a car ride, too. A long one.

Bailey loved car rides. And sitting there in the back seat with her was her bed and a bag with her other things. She wasn't totally sure where they were going but Rhonda kept saying the word *home*. Bailey wondered, did she mean the home where Harold lived or some other home? She still hadn't seen Harold for so long now. Not since the day he'd dropped her off at that awful place. And Rhonda had never mentioned his name.

Wherever it was, maybe she was being taken away from that place for good. That's what she hoped anyway.

"Careful, girl. We're about to turn again. But this will be the last one for a while. This is my driveway. And this is your new *home*, for a while anyway."

The car swerved like it had so many times during the ride. Bailey was almost ready this time, since Rhonda had used that word *Careful* each time just before they turned.

They drove up a slight hill and into a shady place. The car stopped. Bailey looked around. It was definitely a home but not one she recognized. And through every window she saw similar homes next door and across the street.

"We're here, Bailey. This is *home*." Rhonda got out and came to Bailey's door. She opened it with one hand and held Bailey back with the other. "You stay, girl, until I can get this leash on you."

She put the leash on and Bailey jumped down to the grass next to the driveway. Rhonda led her out further into the grass, which was a great relief. With all this excitement, Bailey definitely had to go again. When she finished, she lifted her nose into the air as a dozen different smells wafted by. And there were more interesting smells in the grass, too.

"Okay, Bailey. Good girl. Good to go *out*. Get used to that word. *Out*. Kim said to use the same word over and over again, and you'd make the connection. So, this is *out*. Now,

let's go in. Let's go see your new home." Rhonda led her
from the grass past the car and onto a short sidewalk. They
turned in front of the house and walked up this wooden
ramp. At the top of the ramp, they turned to the right. They
were standing in front of a big door. Rhonda took out keys
and did something with the front door, just like Harold used
to. The door opened.

Bailey stood there a moment, hoping she was supposed
to go in. Rhonda walked in and tugged gently on the leash,
pulling Bailey toward her. "Come on inside, silly. So, I can
get this leash off and close the door."

Moments later, Bailey was inside. The door was closed.
The leash came off. She looked around. It wasn't the home
she'd always known with Harold, but it was nice. Maybe it
was Rhonda's home. Was that what all this meant? Had
Rhonda taken her away from that awful place to live here...
with her?

"Okay, girl. Why don't you check things out while I get
the rest of your things?"

Bailey stood there, unsure of what Rhonda just said.

"It's okay, girl. You're okay. This is your new *home*. Did
you hear that word? *Home*? Kim said she's sure you know
what it means." Rhonda stood there looking down at her
with a big smile. "I know what'll help this feel more like
home. You stay here. I'll be right back."

Rhonda walked out the front door and came back a few
moments later carrying Bailey's bed. She smelled it as soon
as the front door opened. "Come on with me, Bailey. I've got
just the spot for this picked out, right next to my bed."

Bailey followed Rhonda down a hallway through a

doorway. The rest of the house had a hard, smooth floor. But in here was soft carpeting. Rhonda set Bailey's bed down on the floor next to a big bed, kind of like the one Harold used. Then she took out some of Bailey's favorite treats from her pocket and tossed them in her bed. "It's okay, girl. You can have them. Get in your bed."

Bailey ran over to it, laid down, and started munching the yummy treats. She looked up at Rhonda, who was watching her, smiling. Rhonda squatted down and patted Bailey on the head. "Hope you like it here, Bailey. In your new *home.*"

There was that word again. It had to mean what Bailey thought it meant.

She was home.

She wasn't with Harold, but she also wasn't in that awful place anymore, either. She was laying in her own bed. Eating her favorite treats. In Rhonda's home.

And she liked it. Very much.

32

AROUND THAT TIME BUT ACROSS TOWN, NED HEADED NEXT door to visit Russell and his mother, Marilyn. He'd just called to make sure they were both in the apartment. Russell had answered the phone and wondered why Ned didn't just ask him what he wanted to say on the phone. Ned said it was the kind of thing you asked somebody in person. Russell was especially curious about why Ned wanted to make sure his mother was there before he came over.

Ned knocked on the door, heard Russell yell that he'd get it through the door. As it opened, Ned saw Russell's mom come out from the kitchen and head to the door.

"You want to talk to Russell, but you want me to be there, too?" she said. "Is he in some kind of trouble?"

Ned stepped into the foyer as Russell closed the door. "No, he's not in any trouble. Actually, it's just the opposite."

"Oh, good. I'm relieved."

"You're relieved, and I'm insulted," Russell said.

"Listen to him," she said, looking at Ned. "He's insulted." Then back at Russell. "What do you have to be insulted about?"

"Look how quickly you assume I did something wrong," Russell said, in a serious tone but he was still smiling. "All I said after he called was, *Ned wants to come over and talk to us.* Why do you make the leap to...my son must've done something wrong?"

She looked at Ned. "See what I have to put up with?" She gave Russell a hug from behind and said, "Please forgive me, sir. I am so sorry for assuming something that hurt your feelings. You're Mommy's little angel." She started kissing his cheek, and he pulled away.

Now he looked at Ned. "You want to ask me whatever it is right here, or should we go sit down?"

"This is kind of a sit-down thing. But it won't take long."

Russell and his mom sat on opposite sides of the couch. Ned sat in a stuffed chair across from them.

"Okay so, no more suspense," Russell said. "What's this all about?"

"Okay," Ned said, "I'll get right to it. You both know that Kim and I are getting married, right?"

They both nodded, then Marilyn said, "But we don't know when. Have you set a date?"

"Not yet. We're very close. We just have to decide which of two weekends is better. But it's going to be soon. Like, less than two months from now."

"Really?" Russell said.

"That is soon," his mother added. "Are Russell and I invited?"

"Of course, you're invited. You'll get an official invitation in the mail once the date is fixed. But that's not why I'm here." Ned leaned forward in his chair in Russell's direction.

"Have you ever been to a wedding before?"

"No," Russell said. "But I've seen a few on TV. Usually fast-forward through them, if I can."

Ned laughed.

"But not when we're watching one together," Marilyn added.

"Okay, you've probably seen the bridal party where the guys are all upfront with the groom, and the bridesmaids come down the aisle one by one."

"Yeah, like that," Russell said.

"Well, our wedding's going to be smaller. Kim's dad will walk her down the aisle, but we're not going to have a bunch of bridesmaids and groomsmen. It'll just be her and I up there and next to us will be the maid of honor and best man."

"I've seen that," Russell said. "The maid of honor stands next to the bride, holds her flowers. And the best man stands next to the groom. I don't know what he does."

"You might know if you didn't fast-forward through them."

"Okay, maybe I would. Is there going to be a quiz after this?"

Ned laughed again. "No, Russell. No quiz."

"So, what did you want to ask me?"

Just then, Marilyn gasped. "Oh. My. Gosh. You're not going to..." Tears welled up in her eyes. "I can't believe this."

"What?" Russell said. "What's going on?"

"Russell, would you be my best man?"

"At your wedding? You want me...to be your...at your wedding?"

"Yeah. I want you to be my best man at my wedding."

"Me? You sure? In all the weddings I've seen, I've never seen a kid up there."

"Oh, Russell. Do you know what an honor this is?" Marilyn said, dabbing her eyes with a tissue.

"I think so. You sure you want me? To be your best man?"

"Yeah, Russell. I'm sure. So, will you do it?"

"Heck yeah, I'll do it. Of course, I don't know what that means."

"It's simple," Ned said. "Really, you're just supposed to stand there next to me. But there's one pretty important job the best man has to do."

"What's that?"

"You keep the ring I'm going to give Kim during the wedding in your jacket pocket, and give it to me when the pastor starts talking about rings. Can you do that?"

"I could," Russell said, "if I owned a jacket. I'm assuming you're talking about a fancy one, the kind you wear with a tie. I don't own any ties, either."

"That won't be a problem," Ned said. "I'll take you down to the tux rental place, and we'll pick one out a few weekends from now. I'll cover the cost. So, what do you say? Will you do it?"

"Of course he will," Marilyn said.

Russell rolled his eyes, looked at Ned. "What she said. But not because she said it. I'd be very happy to be the best man at your wedding. But see, the thing is..." Suddenly, he got choked up and his eyes began to water. "I won't really be the best man standing up there that day." He wiped the tears on his sleeve. "*You're* the best man, Ned. The best man I've ever known."

"Oh, Russell," Marilyn said, crying even more. She looked at Ned, who was also tearing up now. "Do you believe this kid?"

"Come here, Russell." Ned pulled him into a big bear hug. "Thank you, buddy. That might just be the nicest thing anyone's ever said to me." He looked over at Marilyn. "Can I get one of those tissues?"

33

6 WEEKS LATER

RHONDA HAD SOME CONCERNS THAT, so far, no one looking for a new dog had come out from the shelter to visit Bailey at her place. Kim had said a few enquired but hadn't shown enough interest to set up an appointment to see her.

But Rhonda's concerns were not all that strong.

In the last few weeks, Rhonda and Bailey had developed a nice rhythm living together. Kim had explained that dogs do best when they have a scheduled routine. They thrive on repetition. In fact, they are so oriented toward their owners — especially sheep herding breeds like Aussies —they pay attention to your routines and try to anticipate what you'll do next. Especially with things like taking them out, feeding them, or going for a ride. Now that she knew this, Rhonda could definitely see Bailey trying to do that very thing.

She was so focused on Rhonda that if she got up to go the bathroom — even if Bailey had been asleep — she could always count on Bailey laying right outside the door when she came out. Which was another thing...since she'd been living alone, Rhonda used to leave the bathroom door open. Now she had to close it or Bailey would come right on in and lay at her feet. She mostly enjoyed Bailey's level of devotion, but that was a bridge too far.

Really, the only inconvenience Bailey had created in Rhonda's routine was her frequent need to use the bathroom, i.e. the yard. They didn't allow fences where Rhonda lived, which meant every time Bailey needed to go, Rhonda had to get up and take her outside. At first, she always walked her on a leash but after the second week, Rhonda noticed Bailey never pulled. She talked with Kim about it and Kim said that Aussies were so focused on their owner, as long as Rhonda was out there with her, Bailey would probably never leave the yard.

So, Rhonda did an experiment. First, she made sure there were no cars and no dogs being walked on her street, then she brought Bailey outside and unhooked her leash. Bailey had no reaction to this, just kept on sniffing the grass looking for a good spot. When she'd finished, she ran back to Rhonda who was already heading toward the front door. Without hesitation, Bailey followed right behind her.

So, at least there was that. Now, Rhonda could just walk outside and stand there a few minutes while Bailey came out, did what she had to do, and scampered back into the house. And that was really the right word for it... *scampered*. It was funny to watch, but whenever she finished going,

Bailey got so excited she'd run back inside in a burst of energy, the happiest look on her face.

Rhonda was just about to experience this again, because Bailey made it clear, she had to go. Rhonda had been watching a murder mystery she'd recorded when Bailey headed over to the door, sat down in front of it, and looked right at Rhonda.

"Okay, girl. I see you. Didn't you just go out an hour ago?" Rhonda hit the pause button, got up, and headed for the door. Bailey began to prance with her front paws. "Guess you've really got to go, eh? Okay, let me get this open."

As soon as Rhonda opened the door, Bailey took off running down the ramp, around the front garden, then across the front lawn into the side yard...toward Connie's house. "Bailey," Rhonda yelled as quietly as she could. It was dark out, a little after nine. Which meant half her neighbors had already gone to bed. Connie included.

"Bailey, come back." Was she chasing some kind of animal? The lighting in the side yard wasn't great, but there was enough for her to see Bailey running back and forth close to Connie's home. She kept poking her nose in the open areas of the white brick skirting that ran along the bottom. It must be an animal. Maybe it had gotten under Connie's home. She hoped it wasn't a rat.

"Bailey, come back here." But Bailey ignored her and just keep running back and forth.

Then Rhonda remembered what had happened that afternoon. Connie had called a handyman to fix a plumbing problem with her middle bathroom sink. He had to crawl under the house to do it, right around the area Bailey was focused on. Bailey had pitched a fit while the man worked, barking fiercely through the window of her Florida room. Finally, Rhonda had to put a leash on her and close her up in the bedroom till the man finished.

Maybe she was just smelling the man's scent. Whatever it was, she needed to get her back in the house before she woke someone up. Rhonda hurried back to her front door, grabbed Bailey's leash and a flashlight then ran back outside. She called out again but Bailey just ignored her again. This was getting ridiculous. She was going to have to go over there and get her.

"Bailey, you come here right now," she said sternly.

This time Bailey stopped and looked at her. She lowered her head and started walking slowly toward Rhonda, like she knew she was in trouble. Rhonda felt so bad she almost wanted to comfort her, but then Bailey suddenly stopped, sniffed the air, and ran back to what she was doing before.

Only now she started to bark.

"Bailey, no. Come here this instant." Rhonda walked quickly to where she was, as the bedroom lights came on in two nearby houses. "Oh no, now look. Bailey!"

When she got closer, she reached down to grab her collar but Bailey quickly turned and headed along the house in the other direction, barking her fool head off. A few more bedroom lights turned on. Now the living room and porch lights of the house across the street.

That's when Rhonda stopped chasing Bailey and realized what was really going on. The real reason Bailey was acting so strange.

Rhonda smelled it herself.

GAS.

It wasn't that strong in her yard, but here right next to Connie's house, it was almost overpowering.

"Oh, Lord Jesus, help me." She didn't see any lights on in Connie's house yet. She had to wake her up and get her out of there...RIGHT NOW.

34

RHONDA BEGAN POUNDING ON CONNIE'S SIDE WALL, RIGHT where she imagined Connie's bed to be. This caused Bailey to bark even louder. Some of the neighbors began to open their front doors to investigate. "Connie, it's Rhonda! You have to wake up. You have to get up, NOW!"

Finally, she saw Connie appear in the bedroom window. "Rhonda? What's going on?" Then she coughed. "Something don't smell right."

"Connie, it's gas. You've got a gas leak. You need to get out of the house now. Right now."

"Okay, let me just get—"

"No, don't get anything. Just get out now. I'm serious. Your house could blow up any second."

"Oh, my Lord." She coughed again. "Okay, I'm coming."

Ed Roberts from across the street came out to the driveway. "Rhonda, can't you get that dog to stop barking? People are trying to sleep."

"She's barking because there's a gas leak. Can you call 911? We need to get the Fire Department out here right away."

"A gas leak?" he yelled. "How bad is it?"

"Can't you smell it? I can barely breathe over here. Please call 911." Connie's side door opened. She came out coughing harder.

"I can't smell a thing, but I believe you. I'll get my phone and call right now. But if it's as bad as you say, you better get Ethel out on the other side of Connie, too. I've seen videos of houses exploding from gas leaks. Sometimes they take out the houses on either side."

Rhonda helped Connie down the steps and out across the lawn toward the street. She was wearing her bathrobe and managed to grab her purse. "We better keep walking until we're across the street. You gonna be okay?"

"At least I can breathe better here. Do you really think the house could explode?"

"Sadly, yes. If we don't get the gas turned off in time. One little spark could set it off."

"Good thing I quit smoking," Connie said. "Oh, Lord, don't let my house blow up."

Rhonda looked around for Bailey. She'd stopped barking the moment Connie joined Rhonda on the driveway. She found her sitting just a few feet behind her. Rhonda bent down and hooked the leash on her collar. "What a good girl you are, Bailey. Such a good girl." She started to pet her then gave her a hug.

"That little dog might've just saved my life," Connie said. "Maybe yours, too."

"I know. And here I thought she was just being difficult, running off like that to your place. She wouldn't come back, and she wouldn't stop barking."

"Thank the Lord for that," Connie said.

Ed Roberts came up. "I just called them. Should be here in five minutes or less. Nice having a station just a few blocks away." He looked at Connie. "Know where the main switch is to turn off the gas?"

"No. I'm guessing it's somewhere in the back there with all those other hookup things. Like the electric meter and the water valve. I don't know."

"You're not going to try and shut it off," Rhonda said.

"No, I'm no hero. Just thought we need to tell the firemen where it's at."

"I'm sure they'll figure it out." Rhonda needed to go warn Ethel but decided she better take Bailey with her. "Come on girl. Let's go for a little walk. I'll be right back," she said to Connie and Ed.

Before she took a few steps, Ed squatted down and reached out his hand toward Bailey. "Looks like I owe you an apology, little lady. You weren't being bad. You were just trying to warn us."

As Rhonda expected, Bailey retreated from Ed's hand and gave him one of her best Aussie grins.

He stood right up. "She growling at me? I'm not hearing anything, but she looks—"

Rhonda laughed. "No, Ed. Believe it or not, that's her attempt at smiling. Aussies do that when they get nervous. She's just being shy. She used to do that to me when we first met."

Rhonda walked on the far side of the street past Connie's house. Other neighbors were coming out asking what was going on. When she told them a gas leak, they all backed up. When she got to Ethel's driveway, she was already coming out the front door. Apparently, the neighbor behind her had called her when she smelled the gas drifting onto her property. "You gonna be okay, Ethel?" Rhonda said. "You need any help?"

"I'm okay." She was walking past her car toward the street, sniffing the air. "I can smell it now. We better get across the street, or even further. Anyone call for help?"

Just then they both heard the sound of sirens coming from the front of the park, heading this way.

"Guess they did," Ethel said. "Hope they can figure out how to stop this leak before it's too late."

"I know," Rhonda said. "That's what I am praying."

A few minutes later, their street and the one behind them was awash with emergency lights flashing off all the houses and trees. Blue lights, too, as several police cars arrived less than a minute after the fire trucks. Rhonda found the fireman who looked to be in charge and explained the situation. Some of his men were already widening the perimeter to include several more houses. Another crew had donned gas masks along with their other gear and started making their way to Connie's house.

"Is there really a chance her house could explode?" Rhonda asked.

"Oh yeah," the captain said. "With the amount of gas I'm smelling this far away, I can imagine how strong it is at her house now. You all were very lucky to catch it early on. I understand the owner of the house got out pretty quick."

"She did. I'm her next-door neighbor. My little dog here, Bailey, is the one who smelled the leak and started pitching a fit."

"Well, you deserve a medal little doggy," he said. "Ma'am, could you bring your friend over to the paramedics, standing by their truck over there? Even if she seems to be okay, we really should check her out, since she was breathing that gas for who knows how long. And maybe it wouldn't hurt if we gave your dog a little oxygen, since she was so close to all that gas, too. And maybe you should let them check you out, just to be safe."

"Okay, officer. I will. And thanks for getting here so quickly."

"You're welcome. You did a good job getting everyone away from the house. Hopefully, my guys will have this thing sorted in just another minute or two."

Just then, a fireman wearing a gas mask headed their way. He pulled off the mask, and said, "Well, looks like we're in the clear now, sir. We were able to turn the gas off at the source. It'll take a while for the air to clear. It was pretty intense when we first got here. That entire home could've been annihilated with a single spark. Probably would've taken out a few others besides. This could've been so much worse."

"Glad it wasn't," the captain said. "Great job. Let's still keep everyone far enough away until the air is safe to breathe. And have someone go in the house and open the windows." He looked at Connie. "Is it locked?"

"No. Well, the side door isn't."

The fireman nodded that he understood and headed back toward Connie's. Rhonda and Bailey walked over to where Connie and Ed were standing, so she could bring Connie to the paramedics. Eight to ten other neighbors stood close by, watching the scene. One of them — someone Rhonda didn't know — was making a video of the scene with her phone.

As Rhonda came up, Ed said, "What did the captain say?"

Rhonda told him, then he said, "Well, that's what one of the firemen told us. He said the gas in the house was strong enough to kill Connie if she didn't get out when she did. And there was definitely enough to cause a major explosion."

"Speaking of Connie's health," Rhonda said, "Connie, the captain wants you to get checked out by the EMTs. Just to be safe."

"I feel pretty good now," Connie said. "Just a little headache, is all. But we'll do what we're told." As they walked, Bailey walked right beside Rhonda. She looked over at Connie. She was blinking back tears.

"Are you okay?"

"I'm fine. I'm just thanking the Lord, my house didn't blow up tonight...with me in it." She looked down at Bailey. "How I wish I could bend down, scoop you up in my arms, and give you the biggest hug. But you'd probably freak out and have a heart attack."

Rhonda laughed. She probably would, too.

35

THE NEXT MORNING HAD BEGUN QUITE PEACEFULLY COMPARED to the overdose of excitement the previous night. It was recommended that Connie not stay at her place until technicians could repair and evaluate the gas situation, so she'd stayed at Rhonda's. In recent weeks, Bailey had begun to warm up to Connie, so her shyness presented no difficulty. If anything, Bailey seemed to open up to her even more.

"Guess that happens when you save someone's life," Connie had said. She was doing relatively fine considering what she'd been through. Especially since her house had not exploded. Compared to that, she'd said, everything else was just little wrinkles easily ironed.

Rhonda and Connie had eaten breakfast, got showered and dressed, and were now enjoying their second cup of coffee in Rhonda's Florida room, which faced Connie's place. They were watching the technician from the gas company as he worked on her house.

"I'll bet it has something to do with the work Ralph did yesterday," Connie said. Ralph was the handyman who had fixed the plumbing problem in her middle bathroom. "He must've nicked the gas line somehow when he was working under the house."

"That certainly could be it," Rhonda said. She didn't say this to Connie, but if it were her, she would change out that gas stove for an electric one. Gas was supposed to be safe and cheaper, but it made Rhonda nervous.

Just then a big white van pulled up to the curb between their homes. It was obviously from the local news, had "Channel 12" painted on the side in big red letters.

"Oh, no," Rhonda said. "Do you think they want to talk to us about last night?"

"Of course, that's what it is," Connie said. "Didn't you see Alice recording the scene on her phone? She told me she was going to call the news people about the story, see if they wanted her to upload her video."

"But what story is there, since they got the gas off before anything bad happened?"

Connie stood up, set her coffee cup on the table. "Are you kidding? The story's about Bailey. That's what everyone was talking about. The little dog that saved our lives."

Rhonda looked down at Bailey, laying contentedly a few feet away. Her ears perked up when Connie said her name. Rhonda looked out the window and saw a blond-haired woman, nicely dressed, heading down her walkway. She was carrying a microphone with a big "12" on it. Beside her was a young man about the same age carrying a camera on his shoulder. "I better put Bailey on a leash. Looks like they're headed this way."

The doorbell rang but Rhonda and Connie were already heading toward the front door. Bailey beat them to it. Rhonda quickly clicked on her leash and opened it. When Bailey saw the strangers, she backed away.

"Hi," the young woman said, "I'm Melissa Rogers with Channel 12 News, and this is my cameraman and some-times-producer, Jeremy Cole. Is that Bailey?"

"Why, yes," Rhonda said. "This is Bailey."

"We heard you all had quite a bit of excitement last night," Melissa said. "Was it at this house or the one next door?"

"It was next door," Connie said. "That's my house. I stayed here last night because of the gas. But this is Bailey, the little dog who saved my life."

"That's what we heard," Melissa said. "According to one of your neighbors — can't remember his name at the moment — she probably also saved several nearby houses from being seriously damaged."

"I think that's fair to say," Connie said. "Heard one of the firemen say that, too. Did you by chance see the video our neighbor Alice took?"

"I did, and we'll definitely be using a part of that for our story. But if you ladies are open to the idea, we'd like to interview you both about last night to help our viewers put some names and faces to the footage from last night. What I was thinking is...you could tell me the story in your own words off-camera, then we'll go outside." She looked at Connie. "We'll have your house in the background then go on-camera again. I'll summarize the story and ask you both a couple of questions about it. How does that sound?"

"I suppose that would be okay," Rhonda said.

"Sure," Connie said. "Sounds exciting."

Melissa looked down at Bailey. "Is there any way we can get her in the interview? She's kind of the main theme? But I can tell she's kind of shy."

"She is most definitely shy," Connie said. "But maybe if you hold her," Connie said to Rhonda, "she'll be okay. She's not very heavy."

"I'd be willing to try," Rhonda said. "But I can't guarantee she'll cooperate."

"Then let's do that," Melissa said.

Rhonda invited them to sit in the living room and, between her and Connie, they recounted the events last night as they unfolded. As they talked, Melissa took notes and asked follow-up questions.

"Okay, think I got it. Let's head outside, see if we can do that interview."

"Sure, why not?" Rhonda said. Everyone got up and walked toward the door. Rhonda stopped in the kitchen to grab a few of Bailey's favorite treats.

It took a few minutes for Melissa to set the stage and get everyone in their proper places. She wanted the cameraman to focus on her for the first few moments while she summarized the story, with Connie's home as the backdrop. Then Rhonda and Connie would stand close by, so that at the right time, she could just step near and Jeremy could continue shooting the interview with all of them in it. She had asked which of the two ladies would want to do most of the talking and both agreed Connie was the better choice. Rhonda would've been happy just to let her do all the talking and be out of the shot altogether, but she didn't think Bailey would sit still in Connie's arms.

They got set up and everyone took their place. Rhonda picked up Bailey and held her tight. The poor thing was trembling, but at least she wasn't trying to get away. Connie and Rhonda listened as the cameraman counted down and then began filming Melissa.

"This is Melissa Rogers here at the Colony in the Wood mobile home community. Although as I look around, these look much more like cute little cottage houses than mobile homes." Then she got this look on her face. "Cut. I'm sorry, Jeremy. Let's redo that. I need to drop that last line. Too much info." She looked at Rhonda and Connie. "I don't know why they call these things mobile homes. Do you? It doesn't make any sense. Anyway. Okay, Jeremy. Let's do it again."

Jeremy counted down again and began filming. "This is Melissa Rogers, reporting for Channel 12. We're here at Colony in the Wood mobile home community. Everything looks peaceful now but last night it was a totally different story." She continued looking at the camera for a few moments then said to Connie and Rhonda, "Right here we'll insert some of the video from last night." She looked back at Jeremy. "Okay, we'll pick up from there."

"As you can see from the video sent by one of the residents, a half-dozen fire trucks and other emergency vehicles were here responding to an urgent crisis. A significant gas leak occurred in the home directly behind me, owned by Connie, who we'll be speaking to in a moment. But Connie had no idea. She was sound asleep. As were many of her neighbors nearby. The gas buildup was so strong that, according to Lieutenant Dixon of the Summerhill Fire Department, a single spark could have caused the whole thing to explode, likely killing Connie and destroying many of the homes nearby. But that didn't happen because of the heroic actions of a cute little dog, named Bailey, who lives next door. Her owner, Rhonda Hawthorne, had brought her outside for a moment when Bailey — smelling the gas — took off for Connie's house and wouldn't stop barking until she had alerted everyone to the danger. Here to my left is Connie and Rhonda. Rhonda is holding Bailey, our little hero."

Melissa came closer and the cameraman shifted to include all of them in the shot. "Did I miss anything, or is there anything else you would like to add?" Melissa asked them.

"No," Connie said. "That's pretty much what happened. Little Bailey here literally saved my life."

"What did you think, Rhonda, when Bailey took off for Connie's house? Could you smell the gas?"

"No, not until I got closer. I thought maybe she was chasing a small animal, or something. I was just nervous that her barking would wake everyone up."

"And that's exactly what it did," Melissa said. "Which turned out to be a good thing."

"Actually," Connie said, "she probably woke everyone else up but me. I didn't even hear Bailey until my friend

Rhonda here started banging on my wall. She's my hero, too." She put her arm around Rhonda.

"That was a very brave thing you did," Melissa said. "How strong was the gas smell?"

"It was overwhelming," Rhonda said, "right close to the house."

"There's one more thing I'd like to add," Connie said, "if that's okay."

"Sure," Melissa said. "What is it?"

"Just to be clear, you referred to Rhonda as Bailey's owner a moment ago. But Rhonda is actually caring for Bailey on behalf of the Summerville Humane Society as a foster parent, so to speak. She's taking care of the dog, like an owner would, until someone adopts her and can give her a permanent home."

"So, Bailey here," Melissa said, "our adorable little hero, is available to be adopted?"

"Yes," Connie said excitedly. "If anyone is interested in adopting Bailey all they have to do is call the Humane Society for more information, or go on their website."

"Well, how about that folks? Maybe we'll have to do a follow-up story if Bailey finds a permanent home. Although after hearing this story and seeing this beautiful dog, I wouldn't be surprised if the Humane Society was flooded with calls." Melissa looked back into the camera and stepped away from Connie and Rhonda. "For Channel 12 News, this is Melissa Rogers. Now, back to you."

She continued looking in the camera for a few moments, then gave Jeremy a signal, and the interview was done.

She thanked Rhonda and Connie for taking the time to share their story, as Jeremy made his way back to the van. She repeated her belief that she didn't believe Bailey would remain in the foster program much longer after the story aired. She couldn't be certain, but she thought it would likely run this evening. And since it was a twenty-four-hour news channel, it would likely be run again numerous times in the next few days. They shook hands and she left.

"Did you hear that, Rhonda? Bailey is sure to find a home now. Wouldn't that be exciting?"

Rhonda set Bailey back down on the grass. She did hear what Melissa had said. Both times she said it. But it didn't make her feel excited. She didn't want to tell Connie how it really made her feel inside.

All she felt at the thought was sadness.

36

KIM CAME INTO THE OFFICE THE NEXT MORNING TWO HOURS later than usual. She'd left a message on Amy's voicemail to let her know, she had to stop and meet with the florist to make some final decisions about the wedding. As she walked down the hall past the Small Dog room, Angela saw her and came out all excited.

"Can you believe it? Isn't it amazing?"

"I have no idea what you're talking about," Kim said.

"You didn't see it last night?"

"See what?"

"The story on the news...about Bailey. It was on channel 12. She's a hero. She saved Connie's life. You know Connie who's always walking the dogs?"

"I know Connie. You said Bailey saved her life? How?"

"A gas leak," Angela said. "The night before last. You have to watch the video. I've seen it two more times today. It's also on their website. Connie and Rhonda got interviewed, although Connie did most of the talking. Rhonda was holding Bailey, and she actually looked pretty cute. Pretty normal. But the best part is, after the reporter talks all about what a big hero Bailey is, Connie tells everyone that she's available for adoption, and if they're interested they should contact us. Well, the phone's been ringing off the hook all morning. I've had to get Amy involved to help me, there've been so many calls."

"Really? That...is amazing. And they're all calling about Bailey?"

Angela nodded. "You've gotta watch the video. Then you'll get why. She's definitely finding a home now. I just checked with Amy. Between us, we've got fourteen people who want to adopt her right now."

"Fourteen? Have you been making sure they understand her...situation? Her age, the way she is with kids."

"Yeah. Amy made sure to emphasize that with me. We don't want people taking her home only to bring her back a week or two later. I told every one of them — the ones I've talked to anyway — to make sure they read the section on the website about her issues. Nobody cares. Everyone said it didn't matter to them. Isn't that crazy? No one's shown any interest since she came here two months ago, and now this."

"It's definitely crazy," Kim said. "I'll have to go and watch that video. Right now, I need to touch base with Amy. We'll have to figure out who—among all the callers—might be the best pick. Guess that's a good problem to have. I think to save time from here on out, you might just want to take peoples' names and phone numbers but not spend too much time with them. You can let them know we've probably had enough people call in already, don't want to get their hopes up that she's still available."

"We'll do." Just then, her phone rang again. "Probably another one. Better go get it."

Kim hurried down the hallway toward her office. What an unexpected development. She'd been so busy with wedding details, she'd forgotten all about Bailey. She forgot to ask Angela if anyone had called Rhonda yet to let her know the good news.

When Kim came into her office, Amy was on the phone. She turned, smiled, and gave her a gesture implying how crazy things have been. Kim set her things down on the desk, turned her computer on, and sat down.

"And you definitely read the part on the website about Bailey's age and some of her other issues mentioned there?" Amy asked whoever was on the phone. "Okay, I have your information. We haven't made a decision yet. You're definitely on the list. We'll call you as soon as we know."

"I just spoke with Angela," Kim said. "Another Bailey call I'm guessing? Is that fourteen or fifteen?"

Amy hung up the phone. "That was fifteen. I've told Angela it's time to start discouraging new callers from —"

"She told me. I totally agree. If we can't find a home from a list of fifteen, we've got problems."

"I've talked with almost half of them," Amy said. "There were a few that I red-flagged as probably not a good fit. A few others were a little questionable. But there were two or three that seemed like very solid possibilities. I'll read over the ones Angela interviewed. That will probably add several more names to the probable list. Maybe later you and I can look them over, see if we can narrow the list down to ones we really feel good about."

"Sure," Kim said. "We can do that. By any chance did you call Rhonda yet to let her know about all this interest in Bailey?"

"No, I haven't. But we probably should give her a heads up."

"Okay, I'll do that," Kim said. "See what her schedule looks like in the next few days, see if we can arrange some slots for the people we pick to get out there and meet her."

"Good idea," Amy said. "So, that was quite an amazing interview. I was watching the news with Chris and didn't even know about what happened. You know, about the gas leak. All of a sudden, I see this reporter talking to Connie and Rhonda, and there's Rhonda holding Bailey in her arms."

"I didn't see the video. I've been so busy with the wedding details, I haven't even watched the news in over a week."

"My gosh," Amy said. "That's right. It's this coming weekend. Should you even be in here?"

"Yeah, I'm coping. Can't imagine what my life would be like if we were having a big wedding. I will be taking a half-day on Thursday, then Friday off."

"Got it," said Amy. "But about this news thing. You have to see it. It's an amazing story. And Bailey looks so cute. You can probably find it on their website."

"Thanks," Kim said. "Think I'll do that. Then I'll call Rhonda."

·　·　·

BAILEY DIDN'T UNDERSTAND what was wrong with Rhonda. Yesterday, she seemed so happy and the day seemed so normal. Until those strangers came to the door to talk with her and Connie. It seemed like at least some of it was about her. She'd heard her name mentioned several times and then, off and on, people would look her way. Then they went outside and Rhonda put Bailey on a leash. She seemed to do that whenever other people were near. But the even stranger thing was, when Rhonda reached down and picked Bailey up, and held her the rest of the time they talked.

She couldn't remember the last time someone picked her up like that.

Suddenly, she did. It was the last day she had seen Harold. Bill had picked her up to bring her into that awful place.

She liked being held by Rhonda a whole lot more. But then right after, for some reason, Rhonda started acting differently. It happened once those strangers left. Rhonda seemed so quiet all evening. Bailey hoped she'd wake up this morning and everything would be right again. But it was worse. Rhonda went through her normal morning routines, but she did everything much more slowly, and Bailey could tell, she was very sad.

Bailey kept trying to sit near her and do whatever she could to comfort her, but it almost seemed like Rhonda was ignoring her. Just then, the telephone rang. She watched as Rhonda walked toward it, picked it up, looked at it, and said, "Oh, no." Then she sighed.

. . .

RHONDA SAW that it was Kim calling her from the Humane Society. She almost didn't want to answer it.

But, of course, she had to. "Hello?"

"Rhonda? This is Kim. I just got into the office a little while ago. Angela and Amy filled me in on what happened to you and Connie a couple nights ago. I've been so busy planning the wedding I haven't kept up with the news. I understand congratulations are in order."

"Congratulations?" Rhonda said, unsure what she was talking about.

"Yes. I guess to both you and Bailey. I just watched the video on Channel 12's website. You guys are genuine heroes. Sounds like you saved Connie's life and maybe some of your neighbors' lives as well."

"Oh, yeah. I suppose we did. Bailey was the real hero. I was just trying to get her to stop barking."

"Well, whatever you did was the right thing. Sounds like it could've really been a bad situation."

"You're right. I really am thankful for how things turned out."

"You seem a little down, though. Are you all right?"

"I'll be fine. Is that what you called about, to talk about the gas leak thing?"

"Well, that and also to let you know, we're pretty sure Bailey will be finding a forever home very soon. I know you haven't had anyone show any interest since you started fostering her, but after that news story aired, we've been getting swamped with calls. Fifteen so far. All people who want to adopt Bailey, and they've all been told about her... special situation. But none of them cared. Amy and I feel pretty sure we'll be able to whittle the list down to two or three that will be solid possibilities. Maybe even more. Thought I should let you know, and see what your schedule is like over the next few days."

Rhonda sighed. This is exactly what she feared. Why did Connie have to bring up Bailey's situation in that interview?"

"Rhonda, did you hear what I said?"

"I did. You said you're pretty sure you'll be finding a forever home for Bailey...very soon." Rhonda couldn't help it. She burst into tears. She pulled the phone away and hurried over toward a box of tissues sitting on the hutch.

"Rhonda? Rhonda? Is everything okay? Are you all right?"

Rhonda could hear Kim calling out to her from the phone. She put it close to her face again. "Oh, Kim. I'm really not all right. I've been miserable ever since we did that interview." She wiped her cheeks with the tissues.

"Why, what's the matter?"

Rhonda sighed, tried to regain her composure. "I guess things have been so, I don't know, normal around here ever since I brought Bailey home. No one came to see her, and I stopped wondering if anyone would. I assumed one day it might happen. But, I don't know, I never expected this."

"I know," Kim said. "It is rather sudden. But it's kind of like an unexpected consequence of that gas leak situation. A good consequence, right? Because now we know for sure that Bailey's going to find a permanent home. This is what all your hard work and sacrifice were meant for. Wasn't it?"

"Maybe," Rhonda said. "But...but...what if Bailey already

has found a permanent home. A forever home, as you put it. With me?" Rhonda couldn't help it. Saying it out loud started the tears again. She reached for the tissues.

Kim didn't immediately reply.

"I know I've messed things up," Rhonda said. "I didn't mean for this to happen. I didn't even know it had happened. Not until I heard Connie announcing to the whole world Bailey was available to adopt. I wanted to scream out loud, NO, SHE'S NOT. And then the reporter said she was sure lots of people watching would want to adopt her. And here you are, calling the next day, saying that's exactly what happened. And I feel...kinda sick inside about it. I don't think I can bear to let her go. Is something like that even possible?"

Again, Kim didn't immediately reply. Then she said, in a very reserved voice, "I'm sorry, Rhonda, for not answering you right away. I guess I wasn't expecting to hear what you said, and it really got to me. I'm a little choked up over here myself. I guess I'm thinking back to all that Bailey's been through, and all the hard work you put into this."

"So, does that mean you think this is a bad idea?" Rhonda said.

"No, not at all. I think it's a wonderful idea. In fact, I can't think of a better situation for Bailey than for her forever home to be right there with you. I'm sure, in Bailey's mind, that's where she is right now. Where she's been from the first night you brought her home."

Rhonda started crying again, but from a different place. "Oh, thank you, Kim. I can't believe you're saying this. I felt sure you would think it was a mistake and try and talk me out of this. So, I really get to keep Bailey, for good?"

"Of course, you do. I don't even have to wonder if there's a better person or a better situation on our list. Nothing could be better than for Bailey to stay with you."

"But what are you going to tell all these people?"

"You let me worry about that. You go enjoy spending some time with Bailey, doing whatever you want to do with her. I will be a little sad to lose you as a volunteer."

"Oh, you're not going to lose me. Doesn't seem like I'm cut out to be in the foster parent program, like your Uncle Syd. I'm afraid I'd wind up keeping them all. I'm still going to come down and help out, maybe be a dog walker like Connie."

"That's great to hear," Kim said. "Speaking of Uncle Syd, do you mind if I call him and tell him what's happened?"

Hearing Kim say this was a little disappointing. Rhonda had thought she might want to call him herself. But now, she'd have no reason. "No, that's fine," she said. "When you call him, tell him I said hi, and...tell him thanks again for all his help."

"I will. You have a great rest of the day."

37

BAILEY WAS GETTING EVEN MORE CONCERNED WATCHING Rhonda talking on that thing. She tried to stay as close to her as possible. She had never seen Rhonda this upset. It reminded her of how Harold had acted after they'd taken The Mother away.

Then something different happened. Rhonda's mood suddenly changed. She was still crying but Bailey could tell...somehow her sadness had completely disappeared. She wondered why. Then Rhonda put that thing she was talking to down. She wiped the tears from her eyes and looked right at Bailey, a big smile on her face.

"Oh, Bailey," Rhonda said, "do you know what just happened? Do you, girl?"

Bailey didn't catch any of that. But she liked the look on her face very much.

"You're mine now, Bailey. You're my dog. You're not going

anywhere, and no one's taking you away. Isn't that wonderful?"

Again, Bailey simply enjoyed this dramatic change in Rhonda's mood without comprehending why. Then Rhonda hurried over to Bailey, picked her up in her arms, and hugged her. "I'm so happy. You get to live with me now...forever. This is your home now, Bailey. Your forever home."

Home, Bailey thought. That word she understood. But weren't they already home?

She set Bailey back on the rug and continued to pet her, then she hugged her again. "I've got to go tell Connie," Rhonda said. " She's next door talking to the repair man. She'll probably think I'm nuts. Maybe I am nuts. But I don't care. You better stay here till I get back."

She walked toward the front door, turned around, and looked back at Bailey then looked up at the ceiling. "Thank you, Lord. For making this all work out."

KIM HAD a few brief interruptions but once things had settled down, she took out her phone, looked for Uncle Syd on her contacts and hit the button. A few rings later, he picked up. "Hey, Uncle Syd. It's Kim. How are you doing this morning?"

"Me and the girls are doing just fine," he said. "Just outside on the porch drinking my second cup of coffee. Taking advantage of the cool weather before things start to heat up."

"Well, thought I'd call you and share some news."

"If it's about you getting married this coming weekend, I already heard something about that."

"Heard something? You better be coming."

"Wouldn't miss it for the world. Wanted to ask you something about that before we hang up. But since you called, let's go with whatever's on your mind."

"Okay, I'm assuming you haven't watched the local news in the last twenty-four hours."

"You assume correctly. But how do you know that?"

"Because if you had, you would've started talking about it first thing."

"Okay. You've got me curious. Talking about what? What did I miss?"

Kim spent the next ten minutes filling him in on all the exciting events about the gas leak and the news story on Channel 12. Including the surge of phone calls about Bailey, all these people who now wanted to adopt her.

"Well, isn't that just something?" he said. "Like that saying, God works in mysterious ways. Who would've thought a catastrophe averted would have such a silver lining? Have you all figured out who you're going to place her with?"

Kim smiled. "As a matter fact, we have. And I think our selection will surprise you."

"You do, huh? Must be someone I know. Although I'm not sure anyone I know has been shopping for a dog."

"You definitely know her, the woman who's getting Bailey permanently."

"Okay, I give up," he said. "Is it someone Rhonda knows? Is she okay with your choice?"

"Yes and yes. I won't hold you in suspense any longer. The one who's giving Bailey a permanent home is...Rhonda. Can you believe it?"

"Rhonda? Really?" He laughed. "I guess I shouldn't be surprised. The few times we've talked at the foster care meetings, she did seem like she was getting pretty attached. Well, how about that? Good for her. How did this come about?"

"Guess it's a little more of that silver lining you're talking about, from the almost-catastrophe. During that TV interview, Rhonda said when Connie blurted out that Rhonda was just fostering Bailey and that Bailey was available for adoption, Rhonda said she wanted to scream, *No, she's not.* She suddenly realized, she didn't want Bailey to leave...ever. "

"Isn't that something," Syd said. "Well, I'm happy for her."

"So," Kim said, "what was that thing you said you wanted to talk about? Something to do with my wedding?"

"Oh, yeah. And oddly enough, it also has to do with Rhonda."

"Rhonda? Okay." This was getting interesting.

"Yeah, I know you and Ned are planning a small wedding, not inviting too many people. By any chance, is Rhonda's name on the short list of guests?"

"I'm afraid not," Kim said. "If I started inviting the volunteers, I wouldn't know where to stop."

"That's okay. I understand. But listen, would you mind terribly if I invited her...as my guest?"

"Uncle Syd, look at you. Wanting to bring a date to my wedding? I can't believe —"

"Well, it's not exactly a date. It's a wedding."

"Uh...Uncle Syd, it's a wedding. But you asking if you can bring a female friend along kinda makes it a date. You'd want her at the reception, right?"

"Yeah. Wouldn't get to spend much time with her if it was only the wedding. We'd just be sitting there, not talking."

"That's because you'd be at my wedding, watching your favorite niece get married...for the first and only time of her life."

Syd laughed. "Okay, but you know what I mean."

"Of course I know what you mean, and you're more than welcome to invite her to both the wedding and the reception, so you can have more time to be together."

"Now, don't go getting too far ahead of things. She might not even agree to come."

"I have a pretty good hunch that she's going say yes, without any hesitation."

"You think so?"

"I really do," Kim said. "Well, look. I've got to get back to work. Make sure you tell her I'm definitely okay with her coming. Because there isn't time to send her an invitation."

"Will do," Syd said. "And I'm really looking forward to this weekend. Not because of Rhonda, because it's your special day. Can't wait to see you walk down that aisle."

38

BAILEY WASN'T EXACTLY SURE WHAT HAPPENED TO RHONDA, but something had. Something good. For the last several hours, Rhonda seemed happier than Bailey had ever seen her. And she was paying her so much attention. Constantly petting her and talking to her, way more than usual. Not that Bailey understood most of it, but the tone of Rhonda's voice and the look on her face was as good as it gets. Bailey did hear the word home a whole lot. And every time Rhonda used the word, she had the biggest smile on her face.

It had seemed like this place — here with Rhonda — was already Bailey's home since the day Rhonda brought her here from that awful place. But now, the way Rhonda was talking and acting, removed any lingering doubt.

Bailey was truly home.

Just then the phone rang. Bailey watched as Rhonda dried off her hands on a towel in the kitchen and hurried over to get it on the edge of the dining table. Bailey still couldn't make out what this thing was. But whenever it made a loud noise, humans always did what Rhonda just did. Pick it up quickly and then start talking out loud...even if there was no one else in the room but them.

RHONDA LOOKED down at her phone. "Who could this be?" A little message said this number had a history on her phone, but that didn't mean it wasn't sales. Usually when it was a sales call, she tried to block it after so they wouldn't keep calling. It rang again, so she took a chance. "Hello?" She paused, half-expecting a robot message to start, but instead it was a man's voice.

"Is this Rhonda? Hoping it is. Took a guess from a number I didn't recognize on my history."

Kind of an odd thing to say, she thought. "Yes, this is Rhonda. And who is this?" Although the voice did sound somewhat familiar.

"It's Syd Harper. Remember me? Kim's uncle. The one with three foster dogs. You visited —"

"I remember you, Syd. You don't have to explain. I just didn't have you on my contacts, so I didn't recognize the number."

Syd laughed. "That's how it is these days. Don't know if I'll ever completely get used to these smartphones. Remember the days when the phones hung on a wall and you never knew who called till you answered it?"

"I sure do," Rhonda said. "Spent the first two-thirds of my life using them, so I should remember. It took me a while to warm up to these things, but once I did, I'm definitely a fan. Like now. Now that I know this is your number, as soon as we hang up, I'm going to add it to my contacts, so the next time you call I'll know right off it's you. I also like having the phone near me, so I don't have to get up to answer it when I just got comfortable on the couch."

"Those are definite advantages," Syd said. "But I'm sure not getting my money's worth, like all these young folks. Must have thirty apps on this phone I never use. Don't even know what most of them are."

"I'm the same on that," she said. "I don't use most of mine. I do text sometimes, and I've enjoyed having that GPS maps thing. Use that quite often. It's how I found my way to your house."

"Well, I did break down last year," Syd said, "and used it one time when I was lost. I'd always prided myself on my sense of direction, but that time it certainly bailed me out of a jam."

"So," Rhonda said, "is that why you called, Syd? To discuss the pros and cons of smartphones?"

Syd laughed. "No, but I could see why you might think that. If I'm being honest, I'm probably just stalling."

"Stalling?"

"Yeah, to get to the real reason I called."

"Which is?" Now Rhonda was curious. And maybe a little hopeful.

"Well, I will tell you. But I think I am going to stall a few moments more. Just got off the phone a little while ago with Kim. Sounds like congratulations are in order."

"She told you about Bailey?"

"She did."

"Oh, good. She asked if she could tell you. I was hoping to tell you my—well, did she mention how grateful I was for all your help?"

"She did. But it was really just a joy for me, nothing like work at all. And I'm so glad the story had such a happy ending. Wasn't expecting something like that at all."

"That I'd end up keeping her myself?"

"Yes," Syd said. "But after hearing what she did, saving you and your neighbor from a potential disaster, I can see why you'd want a dog like that to stick around."

"She really did save Connie's life. And my house from getting severely damaged. But it wasn't just that. That certainly crystallized my thinking. But the truth is, I had been growing more and more attached to her with each passing day. At first, I was a little concerned that no one was calling to come see her. Then I found that I was glad no one had and started hoping no one would."

"Well, that's just great," he said. "I'm sure Bailey is happy as she can be to be staying there with you."

"She definitely seems to have made herself at home. So...enough with the stalling. I don't mind talking more about Bailey and even smartphones, but I really want to know the reason you called...but are afraid to say why."

He paused. "Okay, I'm stalling because...well, I haven't done this for a bunch of years. Really, since my wife went to be with the Lord."

Rhonda was liking the sound of this.

"Have you heard about Kim and Ned's wedding? It's coming up this Saturday."

"I have heard. Connie and I were talking about it the other day. I'm not invited. Not that I expected Kim to invite those who volunteered at the shelter, since she wanted a small wedding. Just some family and friends, is what Connie said."

"Connie heard right," Syd said. "But being the bride's uncle, I made it on that short list."

"I'm sure it will be a wonderful celebration. I haven't met Ned, but I think the world of Kim."

"You'd love Ned. He's a great guy. Already think of him as family. How would you like to meet him...I mean, this Saturday? At the wedding?"

"I don't understand."

"As my guest," Syd said. "I'm wondering if you'd be willing to go to the wedding with me, and the reception afterward...as my guest."

"Really? Is Kim okay with that?"

"She definitely is. Asked her first. She said yes without hesitation. And she made sure that I'd tell you she was totally okay with you coming."

"Well then, Mr. Syd Harper, I accept your invitation."

"You do? You'll come?"

"Of course. I'd love to."

"Well, great. That's great. Appears I was stalling for nothing."

"It would seem so. I would've said yes even if we didn't talk about whether smartphones were a good or a bad thing."

He laughed.

"But I don't know the time," she said, "or where to go?"

"It's at one. It'll be outside at a park downtown. But you won't have to use that GPS you've grown so fond of. I was thinking I'd pick you up early enough so we could drive together."

"That'd be nice. What time should I be ready?"

"How about I pick you up at twelve-thirty?"

"Great," she said. "I'll be ready. See you then."

Syd thanked her for saying yes. She told him, don't be so silly. She wasn't doing him a favor. They said their goodbyes and hung up.

Rhonda called Bailey over. She got right up, came over, and sat at Rhonda's feet. She held Bailey's face in her hands. "What do you think of that, Miss Bailey? A man just called me and asked me out on a date. And I said yes. Isn't that crazy?"

BAILEY HAD no idea what Rhonda had just said. But she loved the way she said it, whatever it was.

THE BIG DAY HAD COME…NED AND KIM'S WEDDING.

Syd had arrived to pick her up right on time. He looked great. Since it was an outdoor wedding and the weather was supposed to be warm, guests were told they could dress up fancy — as Syd had put it — but nice-casual was fine. That's how he was dressing, so Rhonda had done the same. But the way Syd had looked at her when she came to the door, you'd have thought she had dressed for a royal ball. "I thought you said you were dressing nice-casual, like me," he'd said.

"This is nice-casual," she'd replied.

"You sure you want to be seen with the likes of me?"

"Syd, you look very nice. And yes, I'll be more than happy to be seen with you."

"Well, okay then. But everyone there's gonna think I got the much better part of this deal."

Rhonda figured that was Syd's way of paying her a high

compliment. He'd opened the door for her like a gentleman. On the ride there, he'd filled her in on what he knew about Ned and Kim's relationship. She had remembered that story last year about a local policeman getting shot while stopping a robbery. She had no idea that was Ned. "My niece is marrying a bona fide hero," Syd had said. "And a very fine man to boot."

The setting for the wedding was simply stunning. Rhonda had driven by this park before but had never walked through. The area where the wedding had been set up was surrounded by ancient live oak trees, so there was plenty of shade. And scattered throughout were gorgeous azalea bushes in a variety of colors, all in full bloom. They had rented white chairs set up like a little outdoor chapel with the cute little red runner going down the middle. Apparently, this spot was used often for weddings, because a permanent gazebo was already in place where the bride, groom, and pastor stood.

She and Syd had gotten a pair of nice seats on the bride's side on the outside aisle, near the back. But there were only a handful of rows, so it was still a great seat. While they waited for the bride to appear, Rhonda had asked Syd why Ned wasn't dressed in his formal police uniform. He was wearing a nice tux and still looked very handsome. Syd explained a little story Kim had told him. She expected that he would, but Ned had told her since he was more committed to their relationship than his job, he didn't want to wear his uniform in something so permanent as their wedding pictures.

Then Rhonda asked him about the little boy standing

next to Ned. They were talking to each other just now. She wondered if that was Ned's son?

NED HAD NEVER BEEN SO nervous. He kept staring down the aisle, hoping Kim would appear, so they could get this wedding started. He looked at his watch. She wasn't late. It was just—

"You okay big guy?"

Ned looked down at Russell. "Yes. Well, not totally. I don't know. I'm so wound up inside."

"It's okay. It's a big day. That old adrenaline pump's probably just kicked into high gear. But really. You got this."

Ned smiled. "You think so? Think I got this?"

"Totally. Soon as you see her, you'll calm right down. That nice music starts playing? You'll be just fine."

"Thanks, Russell. Appreciate that."

"No problem. But...if you do start feeling faint, like you're gonna pass out? You need to know, I won't be catching you if you fall. I could try, but I'm afraid I'd get crushed. Then two of us are going to the hospital."

Ned laughed. "Okay then, I'll make sure I don't faint."

"Good. But really. You got this. You'll see."

Syd leaned over and explained to Rhonda who Russell was and a little bit of their history, as much as he knew. The more he talked, the more she liked this young man standing up there at the altar. Then Syd told her about Russell's story and their ongoing friendship. He ended up telling her what Russell had said to Ned when Ned had asked him to be his best man. Kim said it made Ned cry when he'd heard it and made her cry when he told her. "Got a little choked up myself," Syd said, "when Kim told me."

Rhonda looked over at this remarkable young boy, noticed the way he looked at Ned and thought what a fine thing it must be for a boy without a father to have found such a wonderful friend.

Then it came time for the bride to walk down the aisle. Rhonda didn't recognize the song, but it was this beautiful melodic tune played with just an acoustic guitar and piano. It perfectly fit the moment and the scene. Rhonda recognized the lone bridesmaid who came down the aisle just before Kim. It was Amy, the other dog trainer who shared Kim's office. She looked lovely, but of course, everyone's eyes were on the bride, being led down on her father's arm. Rhonda noticed Ned's eyes were totally fixed on this beautiful young lady. And Kim was beaming as she looked back at him. Then Ned's eyes got all teary, and he quickly wiped them away.

"Isn't she something?" Syd whispered. "I'm so happy for her."

"She looks amazing," Rhonda whispered back.

The ceremony continued, following the usual things Rhonda was used to seeing at most Christian weddings. The pastor gave a short ten-minute message. The part Rhonda remembered was when he explained why he had the confidence that this relationship would last, because of the deep and lasting commitment both Ned and Kim had already made, not just to each other but to the Lord. He was the one who had the power to ensure this couple's love would endure the test of time. As soon as he'd said this, she heard Syd say, "Amen."

Rhonda couldn't help thinking about the truth of these words in her own life. She and Ted's love had stayed full and strong through all those years — even the harder ones — for the very same reason. She looked over at Syd. He was just taking in everything with those kind eyes.

When it came time for the vows, Ned and Kim did something she had heard at other weddings and always wished she and Ted had done. The pastor explained they had written their own vows, after he had shared some of the essential things they needed to consider. However they came up with them, they were beautiful, and touching. She noticed quite a few hankies dabbing eyes before they were done.

Then they exchanged rings, listened to a wonderful song, and were pronounced to the crowd as husband and wife. Ned kissed her like a man who meant it. The pastor said, "I'd like to introduce to you for the very first time, Mr. and Mrs. Barringer." A fun, lively romantic song Rhonda recognized from the radio began to play and Ned and his new bride, all smiles, hurried down the center aisle to thunderous applause. Young Russell walked over and offered Amy his arm. She took it, and they walked together with Russell showing some talented dance moves mid-aisle. It made everyone laugh. The pastor announced that everyone here was invited to the reception. It would take place in

about thirty minutes and the directions were on the invi-
tations.

"Don't worry," Syd said. "I'll get you there. I may not be
any good with GPS yet, but I can read."

"I wasn't worried one bit," Rhonda said. People started
exiting from the front aisles first. "And Syd, thank you so
much for inviting me. It was a lovely wedding, and I had a
great time."

"Well, thank you for saying yes...to coming, I mean. And
the great time isn't over. Kim said they've got all kinds of
nice food at the reception, not just cake. And good music.
Both she and Ned like listening to all those old romantic
crooner songs. You know, like the ones Sinatra used to sing.
Only, they got younger folks singing them, like Michael
Bublé. And other singers, as Kim said, who are still alive."

Rhonda laughed. "Alive is good."

The reception was great fun. The food was good, and so
was the music, as Syd had predicted. On the ride over,
Rhonda had worried a little that she might feel a little lost
once they got there, because apart from Syd, Kim, and Amy
she didn't really know anyone else. But her fears were
unfounded. Syd never left her side and introduced her as,
"my good friend, Rhonda," to everyone he spoke to.

They did all the usual things Rhonda remembered that
people did at receptions. Although she couldn't remember
laughing as much at other receptions she'd attended. There
were quite a few folks in this crowd with a great sense of humor.
Perhaps the funniest moment, and yet most touching, was
when Russell gave the traditional "best man toast." It was bril-

liant. When he'd finished, Syd leaned over and said, "That young man is going to be someone special." He had told Rhonda a little more about Russell's story on the drive over, including the part about Parker, the little dog Ned had rescued.

Rhonda looked over at him and realized...one of the best parts about her time with Syd today was just listening to him talk. He had a smooth, enjoyable voice. The kind that made her wonder whether he wouldn't sing well, too. Like maybe, a country western singer. But he didn't talk too much. And he asked her plenty of questions, as well.

But clearly, the finest moment, and perhaps the biggest surprise came right after the traditional bride and groom's first dance, followed by the bridal couple dancing with their respective parents. The emcee announced the dance floor was now opened to anyone else who would like to join in. The first number he played was *Unforgettable*, the song made famous by Nat King Cole. Only this version was sung by Michael Bublé. Numerous couples quickly got up to dance. Before she could even feel a little bit awkward about what might happen next, Syd stood, held out his hand, and said, "My dear, may I have this dance?"

Of course, she said yes. And it turned out, Syd was a marvelous dancer. He danced even better than her husband Ted had, which was saying a lot. They didn't just dance to that one song, either. They danced four or five more times. She lost count.

After sitting down for a break, Syd had gotten up to go get them something cold to drink. Kim was nearby, saw him leave, and came right over. She bent down. They hugged and Rhonda told her congratulations, and how beautiful she looked and what a wonderful time she was having.

Kim said quietly, "Thank you so much. I'm so glad you got to come. I don't think I've seen my uncle this happy since...I don't know when." She stood, then bent over again and added, "Thought you should know, my uncle hasn't danced with anyone since my aunt passed away. And I always thought it a little sad, because he's so good at it."

"He's an excellent dancer, and I'm having the best time. And really, thank you for telling me that." As Kim walked away, Rhonda realized...Syd was the first man she had danced with since losing her Ted.

Syd came back and sat down. They both began to enjoy the punch when another popular song played. Syd stood up, and said, "Are you too tired to go around one more time?"

She said, "I don't know why, but I'm not tired at all," and held out her hand.

40

1 Week Later
Seminole Gardens Assisted Living Facility
Summerville, Florida

BAILEY WAS LOVING THIS, GETTING TO RIDE IN THE CAR. SHE didn't even mind the presence of the man in the front seat sitting next to Rhonda. He wasn't a total stranger. He had come to the door twice in the past week and both times — though Bailey felt the need to protect Rhonda — Rhonda had insisted he was okay. Bailey finally accepted that since Rhonda liked this man, she would try to learn his name.

Just then, the car stopped. It was still rumbling and the cool air was blowing on her face between the seats. Rhonda and the man were talking, then Rhonda looked at Bailey.

"It's okay, girl. We're going to get out in a minute. You're going to see Harold. Remember him?"

Harold? Did she say, *Harold?*

"Look at those ears," the man said. "She definitely remembers him. Are you prepared for how freaked out she's gonna be when she sees him? Is he?"

"I don't know, Syd," Rhonda said. "I asked Kim about this, and she thought it was a great idea. She even set it up for me. She called his son, Bill, and told him Bailey's story and how she's ended up with me. He was very excited about it and couldn't wait to tell his dad. Apparently, Harold's in bed a good part of the day now, and he sleeps a lot. But when he is awake, his mind is mostly clear. She gave Bill my number, and he called me this morning. He got permission from the facility to bring Bailey in for a brief visit. Kind of a last goodbye for his dad. But Bill said the dad wasn't sad about it. He said the saddest thing was having to drop Bailey off at the shelter, not knowing what would happen to her. Bill said this would be a great thing for his dad, and he thanked me several times for being willing to do it."

"Do you want me to come in with you or stay here?"

"You might be more comfortable in the waiting room. It's up to you. You won't be able to join us in the father's room."

"Then I'll just wait out here. You can roll the windows down. Got a nice breeze blowing, and you parked under these shady trees."

"You don't mind?"

"Not a bit. I was glad you called me. Happy to be able to support you doing such a kind thing."

"Okay, then. Guess it's time."

Bailey didn't catch most of that, but she heard another familiar name mentioned a few times...*Bill*. First, Rhonda talked about Harold, and now Bill. Was that why she was here? She ran back-and-forth looking out the windows. This place looked nothing like Harold's home. The windows in the front seat came down then the car stopped rumbling. Now, Rhonda was getting out. But just her, not the nice man. Now, her car door opened. And there was Rhonda, standing outside holding Bailey's leash. She reached into the car and clicked on her leash.

"Let's go, Bailey. Let's go see Harold. Want to see Harold?"

Bailey leaped out of the backseat onto the sidewalk. She could barely contain herself. Whatever this place was, it had something to do with Harold. Bailey couldn't wait to see him again.

41

It was so funny to see Bailey act this way.

Normally, when Bailey walked on a leash she was a perfect lady and walked right beside Rhonda not pulling at all. But here she was straining on the end of the leash like a sled dog. "Do you even know where we're going?" Rhonda said. It was a good thing Bailey weighed less than twenty pounds.

She looked up ahead and saw Bill standing in the lobby as they'd discussed. She recognized him from his picture on Facebook. The doors opened automatically and Bailey walked right through them.

Bill smiled at Rhonda then looked down at Bailey. "There you are, little girl."

Bailey stopped in her tracks and looked up, pausing only a moment. Then he bent down and she ran to him and leaped into his arms, giving him lots of dog hugs and licking his hands.

"My, my," he said. "Look at this greeting I'm getting." He looked up at Rhonda. "I never got this kind of hello before. Only my Dad got this treatment. I'm Bill, by the way." He stood. Bailey circled around his feet and sat. But she was so excited, she was vibrating.

"I'm Rhonda, Rhonda Hawthorne." She stuck out her hand and he shook it.

"Thanks again for doing this," Bill said. "And for coming at this specific time. Dad's not awake a whole lot, but he usually is this time of day. I just looked in on him. He's sitting up and all set for this visit." Bill started walking down the hallway. "Just follow me. You might get a few stares, or I should say, Bailey will. But everything's okay with the staff. You ready, Bailey? Ready to see Harold? Look at those ears. You certainly are. He can't wait to see you."

They continued walking down the hall. It was a very pleasant, very homey-looking place. Everything was on one floor. Rooms went off on both sides. They rounded a corner and Bill stopped at an open doorway on the left. "Dad really can't get out of bed to see her. I thought I could lift her up on the bed, then you and I could stand on either side to make sure she doesn't fall off."

"Sounds good to me." Rhonda handed Bill the leash.

He bent down and picked Bailey up. She didn't resist at all.

He walked into the room and there, centered in the room, was Harold propped up by some bed pillows, a blanket covered the lower half of his body. Rhonda recognized him also from pictures on Bill's Facebook page. He looked a little sleepy but when he saw Bailey his eyes got big and wide.

"Bailey," he said, "you came to visit." Now those eyes filled with tears.

Bailey started shaking all over, straining to get out of Bill's arms. Bill wisely hurried to Harold's bedside just in time, as Bailey broke free and jumped onto the bed. Rhonda quickly made her way to the other side. Bailey was all over Harold in uncontrollable fits of joy. Harold was hugging her and rubbing her stomach, then petting her head and hugging her some more. She was moaning and licking him and occasionally letting out a high-pitched yelp. Rhonda thought this would've made a great video. Before she knew it, she was crying, too.

"My sweet girl. My precious girl," Harold said. "I've missed you so much. It's so good to see you." After what felt like a full minute, Bailey started to settle down, a little. Harold looked up at Rhonda. "How can I ever thank you, for bringing her here to see me? And really, everything you've done for her. Bill told me the whole story. How badly she was doing in the shelter until you started caring for her. Then you brought her home but, if I heard this right, you were only thinking of trying to get her in better shape to be adopted."

"That's right, sir."

"Please, call me Harold."

"Okay, Harold. Yes, I did bring her home. At the shelter, they have a program for fostering dogs like Bailey. So, while they're waiting to find a home they don't have to stay at the shelter. Did Bill tell you all about what a hero she was, how she saved my neighbor's life?"

"He did." He hugged Bailey and kissed the side of her face. "Doesn't surprise me at all. So, after that you decided to adopt her yourself?"

"Yes, but I'd been thinking about it for several weeks and was really glad no one else was calling to come see her. But after she was on the news, I knew there'd be a flood of calls. And there were. So, I called down there and talked to Kim."

"She was the nice lady I told you about," Bill added. "The one who helped me when I brought Bailey to the shelter."

At this point, Bailey was laying peacefully next to Harold and his arm rested around her back. "Anyway," Rhonda continued, "she perfectly understood that I couldn't part with Bailey and agreed to let me adopt her myself." Then Rhonda laughed. "My friend, Syd, who helps run the foster program said they had a name for people like me down there. Apparently, I'm a *foster failure*. It's not an insult. It's just what they call people who foster dogs but then can't let them go."

"Well," Harold said, "I'm so glad you couldn't let her go. But I totally get it." Tears came back to his eyes. "Letting go of her to come to this place was one of the hardest things I've ever had to do. But now — because of you — I really think I can let her go for good and, truly, leave this life a thoroughly happy man. Miss Rhonda, you are an answer to my prayers."

Rhonda picked up a tissue from a box on the table, dabbed her eyes. "It's been a total joy for me, Harold. I wasn't sure I'd ever get another dog after I lost my Amos.

I've only had Bailey a couple of months, and already she's become a big part of my life. I can totally assure you. She's got a forever home with me."

He looked down at Bailey. His tears had stopped. A wave of exhaustion seemed to sweep over him. He yawned and said, "Looks like this old body has had about as much excitement as it can take today. Bill, why don't you pick Bailey back up and put her in Rhonda's arms."

"You sure?" Bill said.

"Yeah, feeling pretty tired."

Bill came around the bed, lifted her, and gave her to Rhonda. Bailey kept looking at Harold but didn't resist what was happening. It's as if she knew it was the right thing to do.

"You go on, Bailey," Harold said. "You're in good hands now with Rhonda. She'll take care of you. We'll see each other again someday soon." He looked at Rhonda. "That may sound a little strange, considering where I'll probably be before too long. But my son Bill brought me his laptop, showed me some wonderful videos on *YouTube* about heaven. The man speaking is named *Randy Alcorn*. Ever heard of him?"

"No," Rhonda said.

"Well, Bill says he's written some wonderful books about heaven. But I can't read anymore, so he found out this fella talked about it on these videos. We watched some of them together, and they were wonderful. And just an hour or so before you came, he showed me one where Mr. Alcorn talks about why he believes we will likely see our pets in the age to come. Not so much in heaven but in the New Earth the

Bible talks about. Had all kinds of scriptures about it and explained things way better than I could. You should check them out."

"They're really good," Bill said. "The books, too."

"Now, I can't wait to go," Harold said. "Of course, I guess you and me will have to make some kind of deal when we're all there together."

"Why is that?" Rhonda said.

"You know, about Bailey. We'll have to figure out what days she spends with you and what days she spends with me and Alice...on the New Earth, I mean." He laughed.

"Well, it's only fair that you get to see her the most," Rhonda said, playing along, "since you had her so many years."

"Okay you guys," Bill said, "we better get out of here, so Dad can get some rest."

"It's been wonderful getting to meet you," Rhonda said. "I'll never forget seeing Bailey's reaction to you when we first came in."

Bill began to gently lead them toward the door.

As they started to walk, she decided she'd have to text Bill later and get that man's name, the one who taught them about Heaven. She was especially curious to see what he said about pets. Maybe she and Syd could even watch the videos together.

"Wait just a second," Harold said. "Can I give you a quick hug before you go?" He was looking at Rhonda.

She walked back to the bedside and leaned over. Harold put his arms around her and squeezed gently. Then he took Bailey's sweet face in his hands and kissed her head. Bailey leaned forward, and he kissed her head again. "You go on, girl. You go on and be with Rhonda now. She's gonna take good care of you from now on."

Bailey whimpered but offered no other protest as Rhonda walked toward the door. Rhonda backed out of the room, so Bailey and Harold could see each other one last time. Then she set Bailey down on the floor.

Bill gave Rhonda a hug and with tears in his eyes said, "You have no idea how much that moment meant to my Dad. To him and to me. Thank you so much."

"You are very welcome. I'm so glad I came. If you want to stay with him, I'm sure I can find my way out."

She walked down the hallway to the front door. To her surprise, the whole time Bailey walked right beside her, not pulling at all. And she didn't once look back. They walked through the automatic doors into the fresh air and Rhonda realized she couldn't wait to see Syd and tell him everything he'd missed. God had truly brought unexpected joy back into her life.

She smiled when she got closer to the car and saw Syd, and couldn't help but wonder what other surprises God had in store for her.

WANT TO READ MORE?

Keeping Bailey is actually the 4th book in the *Forever Home Series*. If you've read it first, no harm done. Dan wrote each book in the series to be easily read as stand-alone novels. But we think you'd really enjoy reading the first 3 books, *Rescuing Finley, Finding Riley and Saving Parker*. You'll recognize many of the same characters and even some of the same places.

Here are the links for the other 3 Books in the Series. You can download either one now and start reading it in minutes:

Rescuing Finley: amzn.to/1Hn0vrg
Finding Riley: amzn.to/2c7xdWY
Saving Parker: http://amzn.to/2g9vKkA

You can check out all of Dan's novels by going to his Author Page on Amazon. Be aware, you will likely have to scroll down a little to find them. Because Dan's books are so popular, Amazon often puts other books, written by other authors, mingled in the list of books he's written. Here's the link:

http://amzn.to/2cG5I90

If Dan is a new author to you and you haven't yet read any of his other novels (there are over 20 others in print) you'll be happy to learn most are written in a similar genre and style. Although back in 2015, Dan also began to write "clean read" suspense novels. Starting with the *Jack Turner Suspense* series and now a sequel series, the *Joe Boyd Suspense* novels. His books have won multiple national awards and received rave reviews from USA Today and magazines like Publisher's Weekly, Library Journal and RT Book Reviews.

As of this writing, his novels have received over 12,000 Amazon reviews (maintaining a 4.7 Star average).

WANT TO HELP THE AUTHOR?

If you enjoyed reading *Keeping Bailey*, the best thing you can do to help Dan is very simple—***tell others about it***. Word-of-mouth "advertising" is the most powerful marketing tool there is. Better than expensive TV commercials or full-page magazine ads.

Leaving good reviews is the best way to insure Dan will be able to keep writing novels fulltime. So, he'd greatly appreciate it if you'd consider leaving a rating for the book and writing a brief review. Doesn't have to be long (even a sentence or two will help).

Here's the Amazon link for *Keeping Bailey*. Scroll down a little to the area that says "**Customer Reviews.**" Right beside the graphic that shows the number of stars is a box that says: "**Write a Customer Review.**"

https://www.amazon.com/dp/B091QFB886

SIGN UP TO RECEIVE DAN'S NEWSLETTER

If you'd like to get an email alert whenever Dan has a new book coming out or when a significant discount is being offered on any of Dan's books, go to his website link below and sign up for his newsletter (it's right below the Welcome paragraph).

From his homepage, you can also contact Dan or follow him on Facebook or Goodreads.

www.danwalshbooks.com

ACKNOWLEDGMENTS

There are a few people I must thank for helping to get *Keeping Bailey* into print. First is my wife, Cindi. Over the years, Cindi has become a first-rate editor. She's provided vital editorial help, not just with the storyline and characters in this book, but with all my novels. I want to also thank my great team of proofreaders, who caught many of the typos Cindi and I missed. Thank you Terry Giordano, Jann W. Martin, Terri Smith, Patricia Keough-Wilson, Debbie Mahle, Betty Vallery, and Rachel Savage.

Additionally, I want to thank Randy Alcorn of *Eternal Perspective Ministries* for allowing me to use his name and his materials about "Pets in Heaven" in my closing chapter. Even when I was a pastor, I had long respected Randy's excellent research and writing on the subject of Heaven, specifically what the Bible teaches about it. I'd encourage you to get his books and check out his videos, too. For pet lovers, you can simply do a search of: *Randy Alcorn Pets in Heaven* to read or watch Randy talking about this fascinating perspective.

Dan Walsh

ABOUT THE AUTHOR

Dan was born in Philadelphia in 1957. His family moved down to Daytona Beach, Florida in 1965, when his father began to work with GE on the Apollo space program. That's where Dan grew up.

He married Cindi, the love of his life, in 1976. They have two grown children and four grandchildren. Dan served as a pastor for 25 years then began writing fiction full-time in 2010. His bestselling novels have won numerous awards, including 3 ACFW Carol Awards (he was a finalist 6 times) and 4 Selah Awards. Four of Dan's novels were finalists for RT Reviews' Inspirational Book of the Year.

He still lives in the Daytona Beach area, and is still busy researching and writing his next novel.

Printed in Great Britain
by Amazon

19805134R10149